I072E629

Alison Wright's

Erebus.

<u>OTHER KOKOPELLIMA PRESS BOOKS BY ANGEL BRYNNER</u>

Eutaxis   Ecclesia   Exodus

Erebus   Exist   Esthesis   Epicharis

Elision   Elysum   Empyrean

<u>AOLAB active art decks & books BY ANGEL BRYNNER</u>

ZION   HALCYON   DELUGE   BLOOD OF MY BLOOD

FLESH OF MY FLESH   BONE OF MY BONE

BLACKWATER   OVERFLOW   EDEN   ZENITH

<u>AOLAB Travelogues BY ANGEL BRYNNER</u>

BOTTOM OF THE NINTH WARD BULLETINS

BLACKWATER RISING

<u>Anthologies BY ANGEL BRYNNER</u>

FIRESTARTER   FIREWALKER

<u>Grievechronic Revisionist AOLAB Active-Art books by Angel Brynner</u>

DELUGE, ZION, HALCYON BLOOD FLESH& BONE ZENITH

Erebus.

/grievechronic\

Angel Brynner

KOKOPELLIMA PRESS
MIAMI   NEW ORLEANS
KOKOPELLIMAPRESS.COM

KOKOPELLIMA PRESS
MIAMI   NEW ORLEANS
KOKOPELLIMAPRESS.COM

Erebus.

Things don't just happen.
And "you never know…"

But this time you will.

The grounds on which hearts gave out
are full of bones. That speak.

Going back is the beginning of breaking out.

For Love,
and those who think they have not been heard.

Allson Wright's

chapter one

A Banshee child with wild hair sat in the corner of a fortress made of cardboard. She drew pictures of things that wouldn't wash away on its corrugated walls, old-school computer paper and her distended stomach with magic marker. The mud she had been making people out of on the bank of her river was still caked under her nails. Hand prints repeated across the cardboard walls.

Being what she actually was, she seemed small...stunted. The stained t-shirt and old jeans bought for a quarter at a garage sale and then flung at her face in disgust were thick with grime. She looked like she smelled. She smelled like most kids did once they found out they could keep the world at bay by not bathing.

The cardboard box was oily in spots, shiny like huge funhouse mirrors. Wherever chunks of it hadn't been ripped away and hidden in the woods were demons drawn in green, red and blue. Every time she felt suffocated she punched another hole in the wall, as kids that had been next to her until recently cowered.

All the other kids had been broken or swept off to potentially better places where "replacement Mothers" had decided they belonged in the same dissatisfied way they picked out shoes they knew they'd never wear from sale bins. All had been apologized for to spirit children dying after life for love.

But not her. In the opinion of those moms, they had already paid for and picked up their respective pounds of flesh. This thing with no maker any of them could recognize as connected to their own was nothing more than a whipping-child without assignment, one that toast mistress friends would only be subjected to as a pitiful parlor-trick, a last resort to escape Boredom.

Over the absence of time, the Banshee girl processed the physical pain they'd once collectively caused as an admission of guilt. The pain in her head now was the price paid for knowing that they were aware that the desecration coveted was impossible. She had a pre-programmed concept of overwhelming evidence and eye-witness reports meaning nothing if you were a little girl against a mob intent on its mentality.

The little Banshee had already decided that she didn't deserve whatever this sick thing was in motion before officially trying to become human all over again. What was happening wasn't a part of her- they weren't connected to her. They were of no import to her existence any longer. But she still remembered who they were. Unflinchingly she smelled them on the approach. They were the ones she told what had happened to her, last life. Ones who called her a liar *because* her being believed threatened their middle class caste in that particular life.

They thought they could do what they wanted to her in here too. As above, so below. And they had been right up to a point. A point they had no clue they'd arrived at because 'here' wasn't exactly above or below. Here was where things got altered. Put 'right.' Here was Alt-land.

The girl silently played in the box, ran through the trees and basked in the sunshine and mud, her skin an alien brick red. She christened herself "Race Spawner," creator of avenging telekinetic mud people held together by dry heat and the spirit of life in her spit. Mud People that still needed blood.

New concepts glared balefully from her untamed eyes, going soft only when she was lost somewhere in the process of scripting entire universes.

She loved the quiet. Danced around in it like the Banshee she had raised herself to be in the breath of her maker, Aleph. The one the Mothers pretended not to see whenever the parade began. The Banshee child loved her maker, silence, and making things of her own-in that order. But the quiet never lasted long enough.

The processional of the Mothers began at the sound of a bell chimed on the other side of the river, making bile rise to the roof of the Banshee child's mouth. They slinked into the water like snakes then rose upon the surface bone-dry to walk the rest of the way across it. They were always swathed in black as if going to a funeral. Like a small gathering between old friends must always end in some pitiful creature dying for their entertainment.

On their days Banshee's maker Aleph wore black like all those who'd present themselves to partake in the communion feast along the child's particular stretch of riverbank- a subtle visual key to a child with no real concept of days. Aleph did it to blend in just in case anyone bothered to look for righteousness higher than the twisted version of it they meted out.

This time Aleph was in a sleeveless boat-neck tunic woven from blackened palm fronds and lined with red silk, slashed open at her hips and crumpling on the ground around her feet. Cuban-heeled stockings encased her obscenely long legs, held in place by hand-stitched bias-cut ribbons. Her feet were encased in black buttery-soft leather cyclist shoes that rested in slip-on wedges of cork that were shellacked with drip-dried black lacquer, the bottoms covered in dime-sized red rubber non-slip discs.

Aleph's movements were gracefully jagged, making everything else around her seem thick and unclean. She folded down onto the grass like a paper crane to soak up the sun, softly shaking out long coal- black kinky locks whose outermost layer had been plaited into a crown on top of her head. Globules of liquid copper careened towards her upturned face, seeping into her skin. The spraying of freckles across her nose and jaw-line would recede for a few moments, called back up to the surface by the heat on her face. In constant competition for first place visually were expertly glazed red lips and eyes fringed with curly lashes that had been inked and individually waxed. Her skin wasn't perfect, but she didn't care so no one noticed.

If the little Banshee focused long enough, she could remember the things worn by her maker when the Mothers were not around. Aleph only wore one shade at a time, fully saturated colors so brilliant that the little girl's heart would get caught in her throat. The child called up the glint of the jewelery Aleph had worn by photographic memory- shards of precious gems studding her ears, chunks of glittering crystals nestled against her breasts or resting against the top of her pelvic bone on an almost colorless chain, stones always perfectly matched to the colors of her clothes. The only room for variation was in contrasting lingerie, feathers and the fresh flowers she sometimes threaded thru her hair. The child sat not knowing that when Aleph stared off into the distance she was seeing the pictures the little girl painted of her in her head and was touched by them.

Indolent, unapologetic, and aware- she was Banshee's first concept of beauty. The child would zone out to these memories of her maker in the commotion and stench of the Mothers on approach like hungry hyenas ready to eat.

The bell stopped chiming when the Mothers had officially arrived on the riverbank the corpse of the Banshee child had once floated up on, just like the Others. She'd stopped running into the forest to get away a lifetime ago and now just sat in the box, rapt. She could see no lower than their elbows, but was amazed at the baubles, scarves, mink stoles, and flower-encrusted caps with compulsory netting traipsed around the perimeter of her fortress, straining against the spirits of the ones that had positioned them just so. Feathers danced in cool breezes she could not feel where she sat. Rhinestones and sequins glinted in the sun. Real diamonds dangled from ears as fake pearls swam around a racial assortment of plump necks.

Regardless of the range of nationalities the women represented, the undertone of their skin was the true unifier, the same glistening green, that created hues that didn't read logically to her eyes and baffled her senses, especially when she heard them refer to one another as "friend" between their evil jabs at each other. She knew they all reminded her of what she didn't have to be or bow to. She had passed over and by doing so, had somehow ended up here. in Alt-land.

They marched around her box counter-clockwise and talked on the subject of, but not once looked at her. They congratulated each other over the surprisingly swell state of the child they had all abandoned. None of them were concerned with her upkeep. But praises were spread thick onto each other's backs just in case, not sure which of their members was secretly taking care of the child for her to be looking as less dead as she did. Crass remarks in an assortment of global dialects clicked around sucked teeth as the grown women enjoyed trying to out-do one another in the funerary processional, intending with each slur to bury the little child that for some reason would not die again like the others.

Malicious words about malnourished protruding bellies, pig noses and big flat feet were peppered in between envious ones about how clear her skin was-even if it had to be that dark. One of the Mothers started to muse about the sweetness inherent in her scent.

" the little thing's stench is kind of like ...manure-"
"She looks like she could dig for truffles with that nose-" "I don't know whether I should throw a bone-"one started, " I know! Or ram it through that-" finished another.
"How can something *that* scrawny have feet *that* big?" Are you all even sure that's a girl?"
"Equatah-babies be holding their eggs up in there till they're-"
"No wonder they killed her-"
"...to have been there for that!" A lady crowed happily.

They cawed like full-bellied beasts over how impossibly long and resilient the black taffeta ribbons of the child's hair looked as it hung in chunks well past her shoulders. But the pomp and circumstance of cat-walking for one another and the scathing outfit critiques that could make the strongest drag queen cry slowly lost their verve. The backhanded compliments tossed in the direction of her and her unseen creator wore thin and the ladies became rather bored with themselves. The little girl sat trying to quietly define what type of beast they were to her. They eyed her indifferent demeanour after their verbal attacks with lightly veiled alarm. The sun moved to a position in the green grass toned sky that cast harsh shadows upon the faces of ladies.

Suddenly, one of them was actually moved by the unnecessary cruelty of it all. A woman with a clump of wild curly hair and skin the color of a pecan sandy peered into the box and saw a very real little girl taking all of them in precociously. The feathers festooned on the cookie-coloured lady's cap blew in the wind like a consoling breeze hitting the body of a dead bird. It made the Banshee child smile as she thought of Aleph on off- council days and of birds falling out of trees in adoration at her maker's voice. The woman took the child's soft smile as recognition of something impressive in her outside of her dead sense of style and let out her first peal of unaffected laughter since she'd crossed over and been sequestered within this clique.

Instantly intrigued and ravenously jealous by her hoot of delight, the other bored evil women crowded around the edge of the box in search of entertainment. Bloated and pinched faces loomed overhead like vultures ready to strike either the child or the "friend" that was having more fun than they were. The little Banshee girl got the attention due a shivering, flea-bitten puppy who they wanted to both beat and see beg to be fed a scrap of bone with no meat on it.

They all cooed at her, clicking their forked tongues in an attempt to lure the child into webs of false intimacy so the blood would flow faster for the communion they'd all come together for.

The pecan sandy lady forgot where she was and what she was actually dealing with, the sudden envy of her so-called friends having made her heady. The lady purred at the wild child .The child looked at her maker, Aleph. The God was more real to her than all those present denying her existence. The Aleph dramatically caught the girl's eye and gazed off to the east. The child imitated her.

"And look at that! Is that a picture? " The pecan sandy lady cooed and pointed to a stick-figure drawing on the cardboard box, ignoring the baleful hiss the child began to emit. "What Are You?! Deaf?!" The feather lady snapped, her odd lisp making THs of Fs.

Her friends sneered and leaned in closer to the sound of her being rejected. She roughly reached towards the child to begin breaking the bread of the little girl for the feast of communion they'd come together for in the first place. All hell broke loose when her hand made contact with the child's hair.

On contact, the wrath of The Aleph exploded through the child. The little Banshee jumped up and grabbed the pecan sandy lady by the hair as her feral nails dug into the jowls along the woman's neck. She lunged and bit into her face and spat a chunk of it into the face of one of the ladies who'd also planned to lunch on her. Whatever the child caught hold of was ripped open as the god Aleph held the maelstrom up at arm's length, making the child seem to levitate as her arms whirled like a chain-saw.

She sunk her teeth into the women again and again, immortally wounding them with each inhalation of their blood that she took into her mouth and spat it out roughly,howling, blood that they'd stolen from her and her boxed-in friends out of ritual both here and below. The child cursed in tongues, baying like an animal in a tornado of blood and brimstone as she tackled one child-killer Munchasen Mother after another. The Aleph waited to pry the offended creature off of them until most of the stolen blood had been poured into the ground, ensuring that from that point onward, the kabal of Mothers wouldn't return to harm anything else that had made it up out of this stretch of the river.

"Is she death? No, she's not Death-" drawled Aleph at the wounded backs of that particular council as they fled into and across the river on broken hands and bloodied knees.

The only ones left next to the river were the Banshee child and one of the two who'd quietly made her anew after she'd come through, ones who let her be however she wanted without insult or injury. The Aleph was resituating the child in her fort before she realized that she had nothing to fear in the river anymore because she was finally allowed to fight Back.

The Aleph smiled sweetly. "No more hiding deep in the trees anymore, huh little one?"

For an instant, she sat mesmerized by The Aleph, grateful to her God for saving her life for an instant, then was off peacefully playing with her own clay minions. Suddenly the child smeared some of the blood from her jeans across the faces of her mud people. Aleph sat with one arm draped into the fortress left behind. The Banshee's eyes darted over towards The Aleph like a tiger cub watching its mother as she took off her soaked T-shirt and squeezed the blood out of it, raining the gore down on her people as they baked in the sun.

She looked over her shoulder at The Aleph and blushgrinned deviously, chunks of returned flesh still caught between her teeth, the light in the girl's eyes divulging exactly how aware she was of her ability to be infinitely more than her eyes would ever be able to absorb.

"Give-Back." The little Banshee girl whispered hoarsely before emitting the most twisted high-pitched wail of laughter The Aleph had ever heard. The god grinned shamelessly at the loving ferocity of her own handiwork.

Aleph knew she had done well and that the child would be fine if she had to depart as scheduled- even if *He* didn't return on time, as He was sometimes apt to do.

The Aleph's smile softened as she became aware of a scent not belonging to either of them in the air. White light poured out of her face as her eyes rolled back in her head, caught up in the throes of an orgasm brought on by smell alone dripping down into the crown of her head streams.

The child laughed out loud in recognition of what was afoot as Aleph blush-grinned through soft shudders of joy as the primping began.

"...How much time do you-" whispered the child, huskily.

"Just under six and five..." The Aleph blushed as she loosened the lattice-like crown of her hair.

Fully dressed, The Aleph stepped into the spring beside the river and sunk under the surface of it. The mud-and blood caked child stood on her tiptoes and peered into the water, left thumb stuck into her mouth as the air around her became sweeter and heavier with the impending presence of her Other maker. Her ears rung softly as she folded down cross-legged with her eyes on the surface, watching for air bubbles from Aleph. Instructions for the Banshee child to wash the blood off her face and sleep in preparation for the return broke upon rising to the surface.

Obediently, the little girl took a handful of water and splashed it gently across her face. The fields of corn-stalks stretched out behind the far bank of the river and pushed into each other under the soft gusts of wind before they blurred into a mass of yellow and green in the background as she pulled her body into upside-down child's pose, drowsily focused on the still water.

chapter two

The renewed little girl sat on the floor of an anteroom filled with white fog. Fidgety, she shuffled to a new spot every few moments. Blood that soaked through her clothes made streaks on the floor in the shape of an infinity symbol as she moved.

Angry and silent, she continued to wait on God. An eternity later, the light of Love cleared its throat. The white around her took shape, and her anger evaporated as she ran towards the One who'd known her as well as one knew oneself before he'd even made her. With each step towards the beginning, dried blood flaked off of her skin and floated up in the air like gold leaf gilt caught in the wind.

It took forever to reach Him. But once he was in her sights, she would never go anywhere else until she arrived at his side. Her eyes were eruptions of joy and peace. Bristling with news the likes of which one had never seen. But she'd forgotten that she no longer knew how to smile.

One looked through the crook of his arm at the Little girl with actual guts in her hair, smiling softly as each of his exhales dried her blood on her a little more. Suddenly, she stopped running, about a foot out of his reach. One raised a perfect brow in response to the cagey look suddenly in her eyes as she tried to smile but couldn't. The wound of her mouth had healed over so badly that nothing but a slur of scar tissue sat in the center of her face. In shock, Little one froze, so close to him that she could feel his breath shaking every cell within her. There was a soft weary look in his eyes, which were surrounded by tiny lines that rooted her to the ground as it registered that One had aged, which was impossible because God was supposed to be outside of age.

"Little One-" He whispered as the spirit inside of her began to fight, trying to reach out to him with a voice she knew she'd once had.

Her body bowed against itself in pain as she tried to force sound through the mound of flesh that had plugged her mouth. The hands of the child flew up to her own face and begin to tear at it. Moans got trapped in her throat as she yanked and scratched and dug at the bottom half of it, tiny nails ripping holes into and through tender flesh as if it were ground beef, choking back tears and screams as she pounded her own face to a pulp in front of God.

"Little One-" He whispered again, pained by what she was putting herself through with him right there. The child crumpled into a heap in front of the maker, bewildered that she'd gotten so close, but yet couldn't " *No! No! Not this time!!"* She screamed inside her head. *"Too far! I've gotten too- far!!! Not this-time!!* "

She slammed her face into the white ground and came up spitting teeth as blood poured out of her mouth. All that the mere presence of the Lord had initially flaked away got soaked in blood again. Exhausted, but free, she looked up at her maker, gap-toothed, mouth reduced to bloody mush.

"-Hi~" she coughed defiantly, laughing insanely as she spat blood and baby teeth onto the condensing construct beside them. The macabre remnants of her once beatific face twisted up into what the atrophied muscles recalled of a grin. One rolled his eyes and pressed his palm into her face.

"You are so melodramatic sometimes..."

Her hands flew up to his wrist to hold his palm in place. She snorted the smell of him down into her tiny lungs roughly, as if his scent was the first drought of air she'd had in eons.

She even fought Him as He slowly pulled his hand away from her effortlessly repaired face until he grasped her chin and tilted it upward. Little one blushed as One peered into the smaller version of the same set of eyes as One's own.

"This time, are we going to do this *My* way*? -"* One murmured sternly, pointing at Oneself, "Or are we going to do this *my* way? One said, pointing at Little one's tiny bird chest as it shook from the force of what was on offer.

Her eyes darted over One's shoulder to the ornately etched blueprint vitae scroll spilling off the workbench One had been sitting at when he'd first manifested her.

"You mean Do over?" she whispered warily. He nodded. "I don't ever want to go through that again-"
"If you'd do it my way, you won't," One whispered.

"You don't understand how to GO Your way feels-"she whispered back." Your way is why I just broke-"

"That wasn't my way- you hadn't found Me yet."
"If you saw what it was like FOR me, you'd understand-" she whispered, feeling judged. "Why I-"

"Little one, I am not upset. I understand- I just- I have a better way to-fix this-"

"Let me see!" She squealed and pushed past him, hopping up in an attempt to land on the workbench. One caught her mid- leap and tossed her up over his left shoulder as he sat back down to his design.

"*My* way or ***my*** way?" she yelped, excitedly.
"No. My way!" One roared.
"Look-" Little one interjected. A torrent of words poured out of her. "Last time- I had a chunk of flesh blocking my mouth when I got back here, remember?!"

One rolled an eye again. "Because you detoured and missed My-"

Little one sighed. "Look- you are-You're a -well, you know.. .but I'm the one down there. You say you understand, but You never had to go through it!" One tries to interject "well actually-" but Little One goes "I mean this- you know what I mean-" hurriedly. "Why not let me have a real hand at it?!At least some co-direction!"

They fought over details important to His Story that he wanted to tell with her life, and the lives he intended to heal and save with her actions. The story he had intended to tell all along. The absence of Time passed. Finally, after much deliberation, they concurred.

"and if *my* way doesn't work where I gave permission-"
"I know- I know- I promise to find you and do it allaway My way-" she mumbled as One ruffled Little one's hair.

"Don't look too hard. I'll always be right there." One chuckled.
"Now, it's going to be a hard story-"
"Okay, but I won't forget this time- so I can handle it." Little one called as she headed towards the bank of a new beginning on mission.

"Are you sure you don't want a little layover or something? Maybe something to explain the addiction to Hot Cocoa ?"

"Nah-Let's do This- I'm ready to-" Little one stopped in her tracks and turned around. *"Does that mean you want me to stay for a Little while with you?"* She thought inside of herself, confused by how happy she felt because of it.

"Yes it does." One whispered back inside of oneself. Her spirit corkscrewed up inside of herself and then she regained composure.

"..Okay...but only one HotCocoa-and what is it called up'ere?"
"Soma-"
" ...and how long do you think this will take this time and what about the other one-and-"

Little one climbed back up onto the bench and fell asleep tucked into the crook of One's elbow, face smeared with the residuals of the inspiration for Hot Chocolate down below.

After a time brushing the wild hair out of her eyes as she slept, One lifted Little one and slowly stepped down into a river that manifested from the clouded white that had continued to churn around them. Letting her go so quickly punched One straight in the seat of One's soul.

"Must do this quickly before I Interfere- and executive-re-edit" One murmured to oneself. The Other Ones crushed in gently alongside One to witness the sudden homecoming and going.

"She's been in training long enough. Have a Little faith-"
"She'll be fine."
"She'll find her way home."
"Without killing that many things this time-"

"Her idea is crazy enough that it might work-" "If she can recall it on arrival-"

"She always does-"
"And she always does Make it back home too, you know-"
"She's one of the only Ones that do." The Other Ones assured One.

One lowered Little one into the water, knowing it was about to break. The Other Ones began to dervish on the banks of the river, kicking up tiny torrents of dust where their toes would've touched the ground if they could, like spinning, floating tops. At the last moment, Little one's eyes fluttered open, taking One by surprise with the force with which Little one's brain carved every inch of One's face into her inner eyelids so deeply that the ink bled through to the outside of her lower left lid at two points and one splotch seeping through her right upper lid.

"So I'll know what to look for in them this time," Little one whispered sleepily and reached up to stroke both of One's temples. The lines that had carved themselves alongside the corners of One's eyes evaporated under the intensity of her tiny touch.

"I never liked those lines-you don't get old-"
"They're not a sign of age, just concern," One murmured.
"Still-" were Little one's last audible words before her face sank beneath the tiny rippling waves. As soon as she was under, a promise he'd forgotten hit Oneself smack in the eye.

"She'll be mad-then again, she'll forget. And in the end, she'll thank me for another." One thought to oneself. He laughed, leaned over and dunked his own face into the water so that his lips and nose were the only things underneath. He blew an information water bubble at her head that popped on contact as he watched from above.

"You'll know he's from me when you see him-" slid into her consciousness while it was still malleable.

He pulled his face back out of the stream before the screams of indignation began erupting out of her due to drowning back into life.

chapter three

The Aleph broke the surface of the water in a panic only to find the girl asleep with her eyes wide open. A wild-haired Ohmeja was folded around their child, knocked out too, their dusty offspring upside down in his arms, positioned for rebirth. Already, the knees of his dungarees were caked with red clay from him having spied on her while she was underwater.

Aleph ran a re-calibrating spec on the reposed Bodhisattva. His eyes hummed, an incessant flutter of black lashes around two oblong gashes of white. His mouth looked almost carnal from some angles, his left thumb hanging from it, other arm cradling the child. Wheat stuck out of his tangled hair, and his nails were bruised to bring old blood up to the surface so it could seep into the things he harvested from himself to plant. His thick brows danced for Aleph's eyes. He'd forgotten to eat in the throes of manifestation and was sinewy from weaving himself into things she got heady trying to imagine.

"Ohm...announce yourself- " Aleph growled softly, so drunk off the vibration of his nickname in her mouth that she momentarily forgot the fear that had slammed into her as she had come up from the water. The fluttering of heavily fringed lashes froze.

"Get out of the water." Ohmeja commanded,grinning. "Where do you think you are?!" she barked.

Ohm raised his brows and took in a 360 of the construct around him, his grin growing larger with every second that he refused to look at her reaction to the comic display. The cypress trees that danced across the meadow were strung with hammocks of red and blue and green. Silk banners flapped in the wind overhead. Crows called out from the corn fields across the river and circled over the fields of wheat rising on the hills that he had come through.

"Pardon me, oKAsahn-" Ohmeja whispered, his gravelly voice pulling at the ends of each syllable that slipped from his tongue. "It seems that *not only* am I -excuse me- ***early*** for a scheduled rendezvous, but somehow I have returned to the wrong place-that happens to look just like home-"

"I miss you and you're broken-" she whispered and blushgrinned in spite of herself.

"Then get out of the water-" he commanded again, victorious. "Did she pick a name yet?" Ohmeja asked as he looked down at the godchild that hovered in his arms.

"No, and she still has that spitting on mud people thing she got from you -" She started as all that had panicked her in calibration before seeing him there began to creep back in on her.

"Will you please come out of the water-?" Ohmeja whispered, blushing. The air around them filled with the high-pitched whistle of static.

"Wait-No-No - I have-" Aleph stuttered.
"Do I have to come in and get-"Ohmeja laughed, motioning as if he was about to come in after her.

The Aleph looked at the upside-down dusty child, her eyes suddenly very old. Her voice cracked. "Announce yourself to her and put her to sleep all the way so I can leave before you do."

"Sleep? Leave? "Ohm murmured, confused. "Aleph, what are you talking about?"

"She's- I don't want to do any more damage than we already

have-" Aleph began hoarsely.

"What are you talking about- Aleph- what is this?" Ohmeja snapped. The sound waves crackled around him as if he were a lightning rod in the midst of a thunderstorm.

"Ohmeja- I am trying to tell you- I just found out-it's- already in- she knows something she isn't supposed to- and it's triggered something- uncontrollable-down there- all hell is about to-" Aleph tried to find a way to tell him what she had just found out.

"I pushed against my own reality to dial back in here early- what in sin is this?!"

Ohm didn't see the water steadying her. Fire the child had swallowed whole, somehow recalibrated and cloaked remained unseen to Aleph's astonishment. For the first time in existence The Aleph almost couldn't find the words.

"Da- damn you!" Aleph stuttered. "We may have-because of us something got woven into what- she's in down here! And it- triggered this twisted kamikaze- she Black-Holed, Ohmeja!" Aleph began to wheeze.

"What do you mean "She black-holed?!" Ohmeja yelled, trying to get through to her.

"Nothing I could stop, Ohm-" She stammered. "If I had Known- I would have stopped it – they'd-warned me not to inter- intervene-when the construct got a bit rough,but I did- we saw so many kids destroyed on our banks- But they were trying to break her- and - and when we did anyway, and- I thought – I thought it was settled- It was settled. But they made it worse- her sentence worse- and I just found out how much-" Aleph choked. " And her response to it-"

Shaking with confusion Ohmeja tried his best to follow Aleph between her crying jags. Then he looked down at his mud-caked child with all the screaming around her and realized she had not stirred even once. She didn't even seem to be breathing. A look of horror spread across his face as he peered into the suddenly lifeless-looking kid. He raised his hand to brush her wild hair out of her eyes, but the hiss of Aleph stopped him cold.

"Ohmeja- ***Do Not Touch Her- Don't- do not Touch her you -***" She stammered.

His face froze as a term from lifetimes ago began to register inside his ears. *Untouchable* status. Suddenly the air around them buzzed so loudly that the atmosphere seemed to froth up and freeze.

"Why would they condone- How is that even possible if she's headed back down- what- what the hell happened-" he whispered as his ocular tape jerked itself back into motion.

The words fell out of Aleph in hoarse snatches of broken Thought. "She-she's not headed back down, she's headed up! The cloaking rhetoric encoded by the Tryage- she knew what they were trying- and why- she knew the ones behind it had to agree to enact what they did-" Aleph shuddered.

"She is who the Anannke was looking for when she showed up that day- all that incessant death- that massacre of kids for-"

"She's a kid! How did she even get to the zone of the Anannke without being-" Ohmeja began, nervously laughing at Fate's unspoken name on his lips as the severity of the situation crowded in around him.

"All hell is about to break loose!" Aleph cried out. "She basket-wove a retro-active strike strain into every progeny naturalized in the realm- she re-encoded the first string of victims with a virus that set off within each one the actualization of another-" Aleph rambled on. "Dominoes. Once the system got knocked offline, she rebooted, defaulted to an aware. She has full control on every level of her motherboard- direct to wherever she-" The Aleph wheezed.

"Because this-us- and them- are beyond time- they could see- and -they put a spiritual hit on her to stop her before she was old enough to do it! But because of our override, she was able to go to where they wove the dysfunction into her blood-work- rode the Weaver that hunted her here, hunting back through the story the Anannke wrote for her for the loophole to change it!"

Ohmeja sat speechless.

"Ohm, this child has, outside of asking when you'd be back, not uttered anything much this entire time! And nothing more than a howl in the midst of attack by construct interlopers- She's only gone for blood against the construct-"

The Aleph began to cry. "And I didn't know anything-why- I thought we made her stronger- so she could fight back-I thought-" she started helplessly.

"You thought you were seeing aspects of us rise up in her-" Ohmeja finished. Aleph nodded.

"...Until I entered the water in preparation for you!" she sobbed, feeling like she had failed as a spiritual mother.

"All that was written about the Twilight of the gods has begun- through her!" Aleph cried in the vibrating silence of her consort.

"Fuck the twilight of -Aleph do you hear yourself? If they started out by doing- That to her- Whether we have faith in our first intent or not, in our true goal-" Ohmeja whispered.

"Ohmeja, if we stay together they'll find her and kill her here." She whispered.

"If ? Aleph- If we are not there for her- when this- " The Ohmeja yelled at The Aleph.

"If we let her go on, she will bring this all to an end. Wasn't that our first goal?" She whispered back." No more hiding! No more living "in here" because we can't breathe up there-" The Aleph listlessly motioned to the red that seeped into green sky the higher one went. "Ohm, she's been with me this entire time and I had no clue- she has access to things even I am unable to comprehend –" Aleph cried out. "and I Am the first word!"

Ohmeja yelled. "I understand that she has leapfrogged into something she only got access to through our protective coupling- but will you listen to me, Aleph?!" he looked out at his consort shaking in the river. "It's a set-up! They're putting fear into you because They are terrified! You- you tell me to – just go after finding out *this?*" Ohmeja whispered, stunned. "Aleph, they were already gunning for her between births! Can't you see the import of that?! Because they don't believe in things they can't see and they can't see anything higher than Fate! We-" Ohmeja whispered, "We know there is something higher than Fate, than Tryage- than all this bureaucracy that pisses on us and tells us she shouldn't even be able to exist! But she does too! A Human! And they- They planned horrendous things to cancel that out, Aleph!" His voice cracked.

"To wipe away the proof of life that the only thing that makes us Gods above men is the depth of our awareness about our true source! We know where we came from Aleph! Even in this makeshift heaven. We, in turn became the proof of the source for this somehow mid-lined child. And now They are terrified! They need to crush her! And if they can block her from the source she sprung from- so she won't know what she is and stand her ground-they will crush her!"

Ohmeja and Aleph looked across the few feet that separated the two of them as if it were an abyss.

"Don't leave, Aleph. She needs both of us" Ohmeja whispered against the look in her eyes that told him she was already half-way gone. "Th-they are going to devour her!"Ohmeja stuttered. "Under these circumstances- you'd just hand her over to be their -"

"Ohm, listen to me-" Aleph whispered, her love turned in on itself at the thought of her disregard for the spiritual child they had reared together. The path placed before his offspring welled up in her eyes.

"I'll hand her —over to them- because- because I have faith in what caused us to rescue and raise her as ours in here in the first place- in the beginning-when she was just- just a word we whispered back and forth into each other's ears trapped in a paradisal hell. Just a word- that you and I made flesh- that showed up right when we somehow knew she would. I-I feel like she is ordering us to let this all play out, like she's been in charge of this all along. Like she- found us- We somehow nurtured -raised the one they can't- she has become-we, a manifestation of the source? Ohm- She *is* the source!" Aleph stepped back as the frequency on which Ohm was readable filled with static. "Ohm-" she moaned as he looked away. "Understand me- you have to-"

The visual loop of the lush meadow surrounding them heaved forward like an off-track VHS tape. His syllables burned in and out of Aleph's head, causing her to slam her palms to her ears to stop the bursts of pain. Ohmeja's entire form crisscrossed with electrified fibre as the matter he was made of began to dissolve right in front of her eyes out of rage at what he was going to have to watch come to pass.

"If she has no understanding of what *Source* is, what does it matter, Aleph? She hasn't had enough time with us together! What can she call on from within to protect herself without knowing what wove her up so fearfully and wonderfully in-in the first place?"

Ohmeja looked at Aleph as she cowered away from him in the spring, then at the upside-down child he still had himself wrapped around, a hollow expression on his face. He ran his hand through suddenly graying coils of his hair. "Leave." He said simply. "If- if that is what you think she wants- leave. I'll give her all of you in me until you see you're giving them exactly what they want and you come back." He whispered.

"There are others. Others like us. I met them out there. You can go. They'll Help us. Her. They'll help her."

"Ohm-" Aleph cried.
"Leave," he continued abruptly, not hearing Aleph call to Him.

"Ohm, she hears you ringing in my ears before I do- knows the signs in detail- even what it smells like- I don't want to leave- but my heart- she doesn't need you either" Her voice cracked and her last five words boomed over the construct.

Ohm looked out over the water, noticing the red skies inching towards him for the first time in eons."And just- all of this will erase-" His eyes trailed over the construct he brought into being with Aleph, over memories of what was found when setting out in far-flung directions. Creation turning in on itself to create of its own will. "If we separate, it's the end-it -"

Absently, his eyes landed on the red clay quarry used by the child during her creation games. Throngs of mud figures surrounded a ditch, all turned towards the child's favorite seat, waiting. Out of nowhere, four huge crows swept down from the sky and landed at various points around her compound.

"Aleph-" he whispered as what the mud-caked child had them doing dawned on him. "Her- she's teaching them how to be- like -Us?" Ohmeja looked up at Aleph in amazement.

"What do you expect from your own child, Ohm?" Aleph croaked. "Ohmeja, come here. I- I can't- I need you- you can't- you have to recalibrate-" He looked at the color draining from his hands, then over at the love of every life he'd ever been given that had been kept from him in the fiery abode of the gods that presented itself as the highest high. She looked like she was drowning in sorrow. He succumbed to the only thing after life he'd been able to fully trust outside of a source his station disavowed.

"Aleph, re-wire me. I want to announce this to her -as who I've-because if she doesn't see me again, she'll never-let her sleep. I'll raise her up after we've both re-calibrated and we'll go from there." He whispered. Aleph nodded as Ohmeja's smile hurt the both of them.

His eyes looked into what he knew with every cell of his spiritual body had called the necessity of him into existence in the first place.

"I know you spec'd me while I was sleeping-you just couldn't wait-" he mumbled hollowly, trying to tease her like he did before their world began to fall apart. Aleph rolled her eyes and forced a shy grin at the sky spread above his head, pushing the red back a little. All ritual had been knocked off-line by what was about to be.

As he lowered himself into the waters, her fingers reached out to dance across the suddenly graying spots along his forehead.

"Ohm...your hair is going white at the roots-"Aleph whispered. The water began to softly corkscrew around the both of them.

"- For some reason I am stressed," he deadpanned. Aleph's mane had morphed into a mass of wet tendrils behind her.

Ohm brought his nose to hers as they folded themselves around one another in silence and sunk into the river until only floating swirls of their hair were visible meandering across the surface of the water. His mind wandered as the rest of him began to venerate in Aleph's embrace.

chapter four

The mud-caked child awoke to find Ohmeja and Aleph in the midst of the venerate/recalibration construct. She peered in, her mind documenting every curative step for future reference. Tiny, red tears flooded down her cheeks as she was given her only window of opportunity.

She got a handful of blood-soaked clay and shoved it in her pocket for safe-keeping, then whispered goodbye to the All-in-One under the water, her lips blowing the farewell to them in a tiny bubble of air just under its surface before she ran into the fields of wheat so fast that her shadow flew above her. They were the only unconditional love she had ever known.

She pushed deeper into her spiritual parents' construct. The visual delights Aleph and Ohmeja had woven into their unified field for one another vibrated around her, pleading with her to be touched, tasted, smelled, and seen. Things reeled from the pleasure of being discovered by a fresh pair of eyes as presents just when needed. They went careening through her sensory system and settled deep within her heart to steady it. It was the joy that Ohmeja and Aleph fashioned their realm together with that made her fearless. She knew she would always instinctually know what love was due to having been saved out of the opposite of it by them a lifetime ago.

She ran through forests and quarries, and felt her stride expand as her comprehension of herself did the same. No longer stunted by the construct upon inception, child of the source bloomed into the spitting image of the Two-as-One she had left behind to love one another. The lithe, commanding frame of Aleph plastered with the wide-eyed, fleshy-mouthed attributes of Ohmeja. Static-filled laughter danced out of her chest as she ran, devic in motion. Red ochre smeared across her forehead from washing her face in the river and bright butterflies nestled in her hair as if they'd been born there. She shape-shifted for joy, like the wind she felt she was.

And then there was only the outer-world of white-washed landscapes as the limits of Aleph/Ohmeja's weave let cut into the white-light of no-construct.

She ran through the nothing, casting up imagery of her own in the absence of that of her overseers. Vistas that she hoped they might, one day, stumble upon together, like parents finding a stash of crayoned drawings hidden back behind the watershed.

Her mind came up with directives, and the colors of birds and flowers that she saw in her head spilled out of her mouth. She created as she ran, stunned at the reliability of her own words coming to life with every step she took. Then the colors of another creator began to seep back into her view. The skies grew greenish again, the sands beneath her bare feet black. Her heart skipped a beat as the destination she'd inexplicably keyed into like a monarch butterfly exploded across a horizon that had been empty only eons ago.

She arrived breathless at the outpost of Messenger, the smell of sulphur dancing lightly in the air. Upon arrival she was anointed and christened with the name Motoko, a word which translated into *child of the source* in a tongue that had no meaning to her.

Motoko wandered out to the gate and made her way around the gnarled tree-trunks a little girl she once was going to be had nailed drawings to, paying respects to the hallowed place ahead

of time. She walked past the final resting trees of Light Fully

Borne and Food from Above, parts of herself that she wished she had gotten the chance to know before all this.

As she got to the space between the trees of Alekto and Babylon, she completely stilled herself, thought, feelings and will communing with one another for the first time since before the end of the last life.

Motoko, child of the Source built a pyre in front of the sinewy aspens that had been left bare except for the splattered blood of Alekto and Babylon. With her bare hands, she dug out a tiny culvert in the black loam around it. Water from an underground spring bubbled up and filled it. Silently, she laid her shell down on the pyre and waited. After an eternity, a bolt of lightning struck, the immolation she desired, and she went up in flames.

Afterward, there was only a patch of trees whose branches tangled with one another the further up they got to the sun, creating a thatched cathedral-like ceiling of photosynthesized leaves. The webs that spiders strung up in the spaces between the trunks reflected kaleidoscopic light like stained glass as the soul of the source was knit together with Alekto, Babylon and the others into a new child, one that waited for signs from above that the first shots of the war had indeed hit their mark, their official call into the fray.

chapter five

"That should do it-" he growled from above and walked out of the viewing room.

It was dark except for the scrim showing where the target was taken out.

The two bowed gently to him as he departed and they were swallowed by the echo of his energy in the cavernous space.

chapter six

Aleph broke the surface of the water first, Ohmeja on her heels, his fingers still dancing along the inside of her thighs as he kept pace. Renewed and solidified, they pulled one another out the spring, eyes closed, still in the throes of one another, the warmth created between the two of them blocking out the coldness of the construct they were crawling back into.

Ohmeja laid on the belly of his beloved, the black sand around them being eaten away by white glare from every side. He opened his eyes slowly. The green sky overhead looked as if it were burnt, left to blow away like ash. The end-all-be-all wrapped his arms around the first word, willing her not to open her eyes until most of the dissolution was done. Drifts of snow piled up over thickets to the trees, all gnawed at by the white. The child's play pit had been flooded with water that was now black with oil and white with chunks of ice and clumps of tangled hair. Hailstones rained down everywhere but where the all-in-one lay, decimating the tops of trees as they tore banners to shreds.

Ohmeja pulled himself up until he was face to face with Aleph as the white and black of it came closer and closer to them too.

He kissed her roughly, the last he'd ever deliver to the One who'd made kissing necessary in the first place.

"She's gone, isn't she? Aleph cried out hoarsely against his mouth, eyes closed. Ohmeja nodded gently, refusing to pull his mouth away from the love of every life he'd ever felt it'd been worth having lived. "She left so we wouldn't be forced to leave each other, didn't she?" Aleph whispered as she tried to pull away from the end of all things that wouldn't let her go.

"Not-Not yet-" Ohmeja stammered.

"Ohmeja- let me go!" Aleph howled." This is over!" she blindly screamed, finally getting her torso away from his hypnotic vibration. "It's-" She opened her eyes and got smacked in the face by the universe they'd strung up between one another evaporating right before her eyes. A wail got trapped in her throat as she turned on her heels and kicked away from him, about to run straight into the white burnout.

"Aleph!Don't! They'll-"Ohmeja screamed as he lunged to yank her back from the acid white-out just as her first step made contact with it.

"Ohm-Ohmeja!!!!" she shrieked, reaching back towards him as the whiteout of the construct coursed up her leg. The pain burned the insides of her chest and threatened to cause her to implode.

"No!" Ohmeja roared as he grabbed hold of her and pulled her to him again. "Don't -Just- hold on! Us together reads as her here too-" He whispered gruffly as the white began to eat at his toes."Kiss me! ' he groaned against the whiteout. "If they are taking us back, they're taking us together-" He growled.

Terrified, Aleph looked into the eyes of her consort, cleaved to one another as the white-hot fire devoured their visceral realities from the bottom up, grabbing handfuls of each other's hair and scratching each other's skin under their nails as they slid into one another for the final time.

"Together-" Aleph sobbed as her teeth cut into his lips and his her tongue, taking the blood of one another in as the burn-out crawled up towards their brains until they were nothing more than thoughts entangled in one another.

"But what about- safe- help between above and below-"

chapter seven

Not a drop of rain had fallen yet, but most people were already hidden in wood-paneled, middle-class basements. Tornado season.

"You drew on *my* walls?!!" the Mother wailed deep in the bowels of the cellar. "Is this *your* fucking house?!"

The three and a half- year old cowered as the Mother repeated this over and over while she rained down punishment onto the child who'd bruise but not cry, a soundtrack of smacks irreparably tattooed on the child's inner ear that she flinched against with every rumble of thunder in the distance. "Go upstairs!!! Go to bed!" the Mother screamed after bloodying the child's mouth.

"But Ma," the older brother whispered, trying not to laugh at the split lip of the little sister he knew his mother for some reason couldn't stand. "It's a tornado warning- that's why we're in the basement-" he stuttered a bit as his mother whirled around and looked at him as if he too was going to be slapped, which would have been a first. He inched back in alarm. Flower, the youngest kid hiccupped in her car seat, on top of the pool table.

"Maybe the tornado will hit the house and kill her then!" the Mother hissed. She turned back around and poked the sniffling kid in her sore chest. The Mother hissed "When the house falls on you and kills you for drawing on my walls, you better not cry or I'm going to come and beat you until you stop-Get upstairs-Now!"

chapter eight

Diaz paced back and forth across the mottled green carpet in the tiny bedroom.

"I hate this place! All of it- what in the- what was she thinking in coming here- why did she do this?!" Diaz roared into the negative space between the reality of what he was and where she had somehow called him to helplessly be.

Amadeus Gabryl- the one Diaz called H.G. or Dez out of rough-love and laziness regarding his mouthful of a name- ticked off the pieces that had been jumbled together on her behalf. The dresser he sat on creaked as he shifted up against the wall. The mirror atop the other dresser held on for dear life. The yellow walls flaked where it was not stained. Piles of recycled computer paper the kid drew out her island and its inhabitants on spilled out of a corner. Crayons were everywhere. The old mattress stuck out from the headboard opposite the small overhead slatted window Dez sat under. "Have you noticed that this is the only room in the entire place that is broken down like this?" H.G. growled softly.His eyes glinted malevolently.

Hearing the scratchy sound of the boy's voice made Diaz's skin crawl. They watched the little girl try to sleep through the oncoming storm she sensed in her fragile bones.

She laid slick with fear in the center of the urine-stained bed, the huge barrel of a gun pointed at her through the window H.G. sat under, too scared to cry out over seeing it for fear the Mother would run upstairs to beat her. Suddenly, her eyes flicked and she seemed to somehow catch sight of him. He jumped. Diaz looked over at him, aggravated.

"H.G-What?!" Diaz snapped.
"She just looked-right at-" he stammered.

Diaz nervously looked over at the kid, who suddenly looked plainly at him then back at the teen-aged boy, eyes twinkling. Diaz grabbed him by the collar.

"*She*-" he sneered softly in the boyish face of the Guardian he'd been assigned to train, "Can not see you. Do. You. Understand. Me.?" Diaz whispered.

Nervously, Dez tried to look around him at the kid again. Diaz grabbed him by the adolescent chin his spirit traveled in and repeated the question." I said- Do. You. Understand. Me?" He nodded skittishly and shook Diaz off of him.

"*That little girl can see me*," He thought to himself angrily. "*No, she cannot,*" Diaz growled at him from inside his own head "*now shut up about it*" he snarled.
"Get out of my head, damn you!" he yelped. "*This is bullshit! All of this is fucking-*"

Diaz looked at him balefully, regained composure then continued with the dramatic dirge Dez had interrupted. The foundations VayoKahn Diaz had painstakingly pieced together for his charge cracked beneath the weight of what they, as Watcher class Guardians and watcher-in-training, were required to witness. Black leather pants broke against the instep of his bare feet. His toenails gleamed black even in the half-light. He raked his spindle-like fingers through his shock of hair angrily and swore under his breath as he kicked at the air around him. The crosscurrents of the perpendicular planes of existence caught broken crayons up in tiny toric gusts then spat them out in various directions in the room. Compressed rage made the planes of his chiseled coppery face gleam.

Anadhezuz re-spilled himself on the beat-up dresser. The worn down heels of his boots banged sullenly into it. The oversized moth-bitten sweater he had no idea the child loved the smell of tangled itself around the emaciated expanse of his patchy caramel colored frame and cushioned his backbone. Tattered fatigues hung off of his bony hips and fell into a mess of raw fibers just below his bowed knees. Black fishnet tights full of holes coated sinewy calf muscles that peeked out between them and the two pairs of tube socks that padded his feet inside of steel- toed combat boots.

His almond slivered eyes focused on the grayish green light in the room that matched his eyes and the unease in his belly as it seeped up to his face. The black rings around his irises thickened, as if he could smell a sickness that no longer could affect his spiritual body laying in wait for the precious cargo within the room.

He scratched the nape of his newly tonsured skull, trying to focus how quickly the anger that had spewed out of Diaz evaporated against his skin instead of the "empyreanically apt" hair stubbornly re growing out of his scalp to spec again his will. He knitted his brows together and attempted to concentrate on the silent lucidity he felt staring into the little one who insanely had fallen to Earth to bloom. His first assignment, co-chaired guardianship with Diaz actually. She stared back at him, even though it was illegal and impossible for her to do so by all accounts he had been forced to study before being let out into the field for the harvest.

Inside of Anadhezuz, the only thing there was to compete with the hailstorm of spiritual obscenities that spiraled from the depths of Vayo Kahn Diaz's guarded heart was his own faith that he had not only been seen, but expected. He watched as her eyes darted between him and the giant barrel of a gun pointed at her directly over his head. Dhezuz looked up at the window in an attempt to see what she was seeing. Her breath quickened at him trying to see what was there and she blinked skittishly, silently calling out to him in the spirit.

"*Make it go away~*" she cried softly in her own head at him.

"*Make what go away?*" He whispered in his head to her.

Diaz whirled around towards him again. "*Leave it alone, Anadhezuz-Please-* "the Guardian higher in rank pleaded with him.

"*What else are they going to do to her, Diaz?*" Anadhezuz whispered telepathically.

"They are going to break her, Anadhezuz." Diaz barked helplessly.

The one the child referred to as Dez when she was alone with Diaz roughly sucked in atmosphere he could only withstand in measured spurts through his teeth. He coughed angrily against the burn as the ordained hairs on his head pushed out of his scalp in loopy patches and shook with his asthmatic jags as thunder rumbled off in the distance.

"What?!" he choked. He didn't know if the tears in his eyes were due to the atmospheric fit or the irony of being forced to witness the spiritual death of his first charge, but the slowly growing hairs on his neck stood on end.

One of the first tenets learned where they came from was that tears had been programmed out of possibility for those who operated on his current plane of existence.

"Dez..." Vayo Kahn Diaz whispered softly, using her name for him, trying to find some gentle space within his own harshness to speak to Anadhezuz from, knowing what this was going to do to the boy due to what watching helplessly had done to him.

"No-" Anadhezuz spat out. "They began killing her long before anything they could do in this death today. But I know she clearly saw me-so maybe-" Lightning cracked some 20 miles away.

"H.G! How many- You imagined that!" Diaz flew into a rage as if each word had cut into a different chunk of soul. "She can't see YOU!!! She can't see us! There's nothing we can do but watch! It's our lot- your New lot and mines for-this twisted eternity-" He panted wildly, bewildering Anadhezuz, who had no clue it was for the girl's own good.

The abysmal depths of love yanked away from Vayo Kahn Diaz across forevers finally reached critical mass in the stuffy room. He crumbled to the floor as if hit by a bullet in the chest. His thick mouth ripped open in pain screaming so violently that dogs howled outside in the electrical storm. Shards of light exploded from his chest, roughly yanking Anadhezuz up and flinging him against the mirror over the other dresser with such ferocity that both his spirit and the glass cracked.

H.G. cowered against the broken mirror, Diaz's last words swirling around him like madness as half of what was left of

him stumbled down towards the entity he had grown to love like a father never had above or below and collapsed against him.

Vayo Kahn Diaz continued to howl from the spiritual hit he'd taken for the little girl.

What was left of Anadhezuz's afterlife as he had known it blindly cringed against the mirror, stunned into shock by tears that couldn't be coursing down his cheeks until he heard the little girl's sobs.

"I'm going to get in trouble for that too- " she wailed softly as each syllable stumbled atop another. His head whipped towards her and saw her stiffen at the sound of the cocking of the large gun now audible to him as it filled the room. A second gigantic bullet exploded out of the chamber of the gun he too could now see. Disoriented, he flung his spirit across the room onto the little girl, shielding her, the second bullet tearing into his back instead of her.

The strength of the blast he blocked slammed the bed roughly into the wall and cracked the headboard behind her. The air around them buzzed as they looked at each other, bewildered. The little girl reached a tiny hand up to touch his face as his spirit splintered from the visuals of a fifteen-year-old lost boy that had committed suicide on a couch in Jersey to that of a scared, almost six-year old boy.

"What-what happened?!" They whispered in unison as the 15-year old vanished like a ghost, leaving a scared little boy staring at an even more terrified little girl. A torrential downpour started outside.

"What The Hell Was That?!" The Mother roared from downstairs in reaction to all the noise.

"Run! Hide!" the little girl squealed to the boy.

"Don't let her see you!" she shoved him away from her and hugged her knees to her chest.
"Run where?!" he howled.
"I dont know! Go! Please!" she hissed, wet-faced.

The little boy turned frantically. The greenish light from the tornado storm hit the cracked mirror in a way that drew him to it. Cagily, he scrambled up onto the dresser, held his breath with faith and slipped through the surface of the mirror just as the Mother slammed open the bedroom door.

The cracks in the mirror healed themselves a split second before she looked at it. The little boy ducked down so that only one eye was visible in the lower corner of the mirror and watched.

The terrified little girl pressed against the broken headboard, praying that it would heal like the mirror, that the Mother wouldn't see. A wet ring began to spread underneath the petrified child as she lost control of her bladder.

Furious, unaware of the broken headboard resituating itself in front of her, the Mother grabbed the frightened child by the face and shoved it into her own urine.

"You disgusting little-" she hissed but froze at the sudden sound of a car pulling into the driveway. Her grip loosened and she narrowed her eyes as a fierce look of hope spread across the little girl's wet face. Her Father. The mother stepped back from the bed and pointed warningly at the child.

"Not a word- you hear me? Not a –" The Mother backed out of the room and slammed the bedroom door shut. The little boy stood frozen on the other side of the mirror as the little girl curled up into a ball and cried herself to sleep.

chapter nine

"I'm not supposed to talk about it-but I have to." Diaz muttered. "Just start from the-beginning,"Comptroller IIrys said gingerly.

She knew he'd been taken off the field eons ago due to an incident that had collapsed his cage, burning off half of the Guardian he'd had in training alongside him under the radar. She resisted the desire to pat his hand. To do so could've led to another blow, this time officially from the Tryage, from which he might not recover. He'd been through enough.

His last sight of what was left of Anadhezuz Gabryl was the being fighting to tear itself in two along the schism Vayo Kahn's censure and subsequent cage collapse had caused as Vayo was ordered to de-briefing regarding the small child who had miraculously survived the spiritual hit Sector had no official record of having mandated. The half-life he had brought back up Jacob's Ladder in his arms like he were his own son was never seen or spoke of again in the realm.

The beyond Untouchable aspect of Sr. VayoKahn Diaz was obvious. The cloaking suit of his senses purred, making white-noise through which he was able to speak candidly to Comptroller IIrys during the session.

"Guess it started with the pictures. She had to have been about two. She had been drawing since she could grasp anything in her hands with me peering over her shoulder, trying to remember what it felt like to hold a crayon."

"I remember when her eyes started following me around the room, when she started eavesdropping on me as obviously as I had been nosing in on her... But around her second birthday-which was her third according to me, she started holding up the pictures in rooms she'd been put into alone as punishment. It took a moment for me to get that she was holding them up for me to see. And a second more to get it was because she didn't like me looking over her shoulder like I did."

He cleared his throat.

"When the abuse started, she was three by their clocks. She started talking to me on her plane because of it. She almost dared me not to speak back. She asked me what she'd done to make them want to kill her. Just like that. The way other kids her age asked what color an orange was. She kept asking me if I would take her to where she was really from, daring me to say it was where she was. She kept talking aloud to me like she could hear my trying not to answer her, as if she knew I was listening with everything I had, trying to find a way to legally reply. Because you know we're not supposed-" His jaw clenched.

"The first time I *felt* wetness on my cheeks was the day we got back from the house of the aunt who baby-sat- who repeatedly raped her, rammed her face into her crotch, told her she was destroying her, and that nobody gave a fuck about her either, that she wasn't allowed to wash anything off of her, that she wasn't so special. She had stared listlessly at me in a corner in her room, then ran to the bathroom and puked until she thought she was destroyed, just like her aunt said. I watched this little kid catch sight of herself in the mirror, shocked she was still there at first. Then she looked at me, watching her, this weird mix of shame, comprehension and supernatural defiance in her eyes. Then she spoke. To me. Telepathically. On our frequency."

Comptroller Yris stiffened then shook it off before the sectoring surveillance system could pick up the flux in her energy lines.

Kahn continued."She said I'm asking you one more time-"
teeth bared.

"So I answered her. Stunned. And I –I reached down – I knelt
and she- hugged me. This-" he hissed softly, gesturing towards
his spiritual body. I-I picked her up and held her.& I don't
know if the tears were hers or mine, but– I completely
registered to her. Physically."

He paused. "I told her that I was from where she came from.
And that she knew more than me because she could see where
she was and me at the same time. She told me she couldn't see
me but she could feel-and hear who I was through her eyes.
When I took her there, she asked me why the sky was red. I
told her the colors turned in on themselves where she currently
was stationed."

"That explains the balls." she had whispered into my hair.
"What balls?" I had said absently, shuffling her in my arms like
I had seen humans do with heavy groceries since I couldn't
recall how it was supposed to feel to hold a child even as I did
it."

"When the lights go out at night, everything breaks into these
green, blue, and red little balls-"

"I had been there silently for years, but suddenly if she didn't
acknowledge me I felt as if I would go crazy. You don't know
how it feels to be seen like that. After eons of being told it was
impossible. *She* could hear me with her eyes. *She* knew more
of what I looked like than I did. And I wasn't the only one she
could see. She could see all of Us- everybody's angels! As they
hovered next to strollers or hobbled next to canes, the entire
hierarchy seemed to stand up a little straighter whenever she
was near their posts in case she'd happen to look in their
direction. The ones she looked at pledged their allegiance to

her for eternity in silent gratitude for being seen."

"The older she got, the more detached from it all she became. The abuse and the second sight- her ability to see us- did something else to her eyes regarding the "real" people, places and things around her. The adults felt stripped naked, ugly, as if all their hidden cruelties, the twisted things done and or sanctioned had left horrible blisters over their skin that they only felt in her presence. The eczema she'd been born with would flare up whenever she was forced to stay near people who meant her any harm, as if she was allergic."

"Then the test scores started coming in. Made people nervous who had things to hide, things that they wanted to keep doing. So they told other adults she was a liar just in case.

"Human Years whirled by like this. Comprehension tests with perfect scores, alarmed adults. Her pulling herself farther away from them. Closer to me and others like me, like she could smell what fear made humans capable of doing, before they could even think to do it."

"She was very lonely. Would dumb it down- all nines and one eight on scores- and the adults would back off. Some.

Except for when the little boy who she could hear with her eyes like she heard me came around. Except he wasn't like Us. He was like her, only very far away."

He stopped and stared off into space, his expertly applied copper coloring fading to white as he wrestled with what was trying to come out of him. "He kind of reminded me of H.G. Anadhezuz. The half-life, as a boy. The one I lost. The one I- only even smaller, if you can imagine. But he was another one like her, out there somehow, eyes ripped open."

"I think that's enough for today, Diaz. You're losing your color-" Comptroller IIrys said, visibly shaken by his account. She pressed a button and the panels of the wall shifted to reveal the wall of windows that looked out onto the red sky of the Empyrean.

"No- I really need to talk-" Kahn interjected. "I don't know what else to do but-"

"Look, Kahn-" IIrys said softly, surreptitiously stretching a hand under the table they sat at to grab his. He started at her touching him. She blinked to let him know. *"I understand how you...feel."* She said telepathically. He blinked back at her in surprise. "This session is over. According to Tryage, which as we both know documents these "helps," we have another one scheduled soon. Understand? "IIrys said curtly, giving his hand a tiny cloaked squeeze as she did.

"Understood." He said, clearing his throat.
"Now you must know, Sr. Vayo Kahn Diaz, that as one of our realms most prized Master Builders, your spiritual state is very important to the Empyrean."

"And the Tryage has taken very special measures to have you back in, shall we say, tip-top shape at the earliest possible." Comptroller IIrys continued stiffly, squeezing his fingers out of sight. He showed no signs of the cloaked contact. She slid her hand out of his grasp, stood up to go, then turned and extended her hand woodenly towards him on tape for the first time. A red flag waved in front of the Watchers on duty.

"what is she doing" One not used to thinking thought.

"Never- mind. it's nothing-" The other Watcher replied to the in-utero streaming system that VayoKahn Diaz himself had constructed, consciously turning a blind eye to the line that had been crossed to save the man who was currently their cloaked

proof of life.

He grabbed at her hand as if it were a life preserver, then smiled as he consciously missed contact as per norm. "Good day, Kahn." She leaned in and whispered into his ear in tongues. *"Malak-toh been-day-rof-nah"*

"Until the next session." He stated for the record. Comptroller IIrys turned to go, then paused. "What direction are you going?" She asked casually.

"To the pools in the Empyrean gardens. I need to regulate my senses." Kahn replied simply.

"I'm going in that direction too..." Comptroller IIrys stated. "How nice for you, Good Day." Kahn replied, dismissing her company. He walked into the changing room to take off the suit encrusted with recording receptors.

chapter ten

The fighting waged on downstairs. Like a soldier suffering ptsd in the calm between battles in a war zone, Anukai was numb to the catastrophes that played out between her parents on a daily basis. She had analyzed the situation. It wasn't logical to care.

At eight years old she was five foot two, with wild, thick hair she hated because it had to be done by the Mother downstairs hell-bent on treating Anukai like a POW as soon as the Father was out of dodge. When he was around Anukai waited. Behind the door of the second floor bathroom until the fight was done and the doors slammed.

Mostly the Mother went out to shop or bitch with the married, barren woman next door who was secretly trying to sleep with her husband, but sometimes she stormed upstairs, which is why the child hid.

The Mother stomped up the stairs, curse words frothing at the corners of her mouth. "Who the fuck does he think he is?! THEY are not my friends?" she seethed. "YOU'RE not my friend, you Asshole!!" she screamed, inches from where Anukai had hidden herself. There was no reply back which pissed her off even more. Whenever it was too quiet, the mother knew Anukai was somewhere around. She narrowed her eyes.

"I know you're somewhere around here-I can *smell* you, Anukai! You smell like a dirty old woman! That's why I tell you to wash up, because you stink! You hear me?!"

Anukai's breath hitched in her chest. It wasn't the first time she'd received the tail end of the mother's instincts to maul.

She was numb. Smart enough to understand the word "factions" when the spirit that took care of her had knocked a book off the shelf in the library and it had fallen open to it. And most importantly, she knew the Father was trying to drive her Mother crazy because he wanted to be a dictator somewhere and couldn't be one out in the world. He had told her as much during their time in the "Club."

But today, tears spilled down her cheeks because after all those years of being told by her mother that she stunk when she didn't, or did after being baby-sat, which was ignored all those times, that day three girls in class who were mad that Jackson had sat next to her, not them that morning chanted "Anukai the Giant Stink" all the way home. And she couldn't say anything because after all those times of being face to face with the stench of her aunt, what "stunk" meant in her frame of reference ran rip shod over her.

The Mother smelled the salt in the air from her tears like blood. "Yeah, I know-you're Crying? Keep hiding. Waiting for your Daddy to make it all better and let you into "the club" I'm not allowed into! Fuck him! And fuck you too! You filthy little-" She snarled then stormed back downstairs and out the side door as the "father" headed up from the kitchen. Anukai wiped away her tears on the hem of her Spiderman tee-shirt.

"I know I don't stink! I know I don't" she whispered harshly to herself and the Spirit that had been sitting by her the whole time. *"But...he's the only one who'd tell me if I did-"* she thought to herself.

Her mother gunned the engine as her father crossed the threshold into her parents' room. Anukai heard the door creak shut but not latch.

It was 4 o'clock. Right on time. The voice of Leonard Nimoy plugged the silence in the house.

"...and This is...**In Search of.**"
Anukai flew in and sat on the end of the king-sized bed closest to the television. She couldn't even look back at the father because Spock was talking. And she liked Spock. He made sense. Sense that overrode the insanity she was living in.

"Did Atlantis really exist? Who is Edgar Cayce, and what did he say about Bimini Road before he..."

"Is she gone for good?" Anukai called out ten minutes into the show.
"Probably not," he laughed. "Did she hit you?" he asked warily.

Not this time. Anukai thought to herself as she softly shook her head no. Then, overcome, she cried out "Daddy can you smell me?!"

"WHAT?" he asked, bewildered.

Anukai looked over her shoulder balefully to see if he was shocked for real."Can you smell me from there!!?" she howled and started to cry.

"..why, did you fart?" he chuckled.
"No!" she wailed, momentarily inconsolable.
"I just did-" As soon as he said it, the smell put her in a headlock.

"Ewwwwwww~!What did you eat?!?!" Anukai howled, tears forgotten in grossed out guffaws of laughter.

"Pork and Beans, Grits, sausage, Sanka, collard greens and some eggs-" He ticked off the ingredients to his most recent feast as it laid smelly siege to the entire second floor.

"You probably put it all in one bowl too!" she fussed.

"That's how it's going to end up anyway!!" He laughed. "Look, In search of is back on-" he whispered. They eased back into silence as Nimoy spoke.

"Do you believe in Atlantis, daddy?" Anukai whispered.

"Atlantis? Yeah, but that's not its real name-they spelling it wrong to trip folks up-That's why they cant ever find stuff-- it's Altand, but you say it like you siddity-Alt~Lahnduh~" he whispered "Now shush."

She hesitated. "Daddy, she told me I stink- "
"She always does that Anuk,"
"But today- they said it at school too-" she mumbled as tears started to roll down her cheeks.

"That doesn't make it true." He paused for a minute. "You don't stink. Even when you stink, you don't stink. I'd tell you when you stink. I'd be proud-"

Her father's look of bewilderment spread across her face. She swiveled around to look at him suspiciously "Why?!" she asked hotly.

"Because it'd mean you were finally eating right!" he chuckled.

She cut her eyes at him then laughed."Wait a minute-" she mumbled. Her "father" grinned at her like lilbabyjesus as she sniffed the air apprehensively. "Ew~oh gawd!!! Smells like something died in you!!!" Anukai laughed as she fell off the edge of the bed, wounded.

"You like being in the club, you gotta pay your dues, kid-"
"What is wrong with your belly?! You smell like you ate roadkill!"

"Be quiet, In search of is back on-" he hissed and farted again.
"Oh God! That's it- I'm leaving!-" she screamed.
"Anukai! Anukai!!!" Her father called after her.
"What?" she whispered as she made her way to the door, holding her nose dramatically when she finally looked back at him.

"Next time they tell you that, that is what you do. Fart'em out of - Any of them. Including ya momma. Okay?" He laughed.

"Okay" she laughed back.
"Especially ya momma. Only thing that'll make her stop- is when I-you know~" He blushed. " And you picked my intestines, so that's built-in weaponry." He paused and tilted his head so he could truly see her. "You cool?"

"Yeah, I'm cool." she whispered.
"Still mad at me?"
She sighed melodramatically."Noooo~"
"Good. Now shut the door and don't let nobody else into the club."

She did as she was told.

chapter eleven

"What do we do with them?"
The watchers assigned to the half-life shifted so they could see the now destroyed construct spread out around them.

The two that the untouchable half-life had splintered into lunged at one another and brawled until ethereally reinforced skins broke again and flooded the construct with spiritual blood that supposedly had already been drained from the two of the him. Twice.

They fought through ages that coursed back and forth over the surfaces of their skins like the sun playing on water, howling as they tried to beat the rest of themselves out of each other to no avail. Teenaged to childlike and back, the only time the two aspects of oneself had any sense of unified purpose was when they turned and ripped to shreds any ANC genomic gearhead on watch that dared enter the fray alone.

"Anad-" the latest ANC being pulled apart wheezed, "Hezuz!! Stop this! Stop!" To no avail.

A cluster of bruised Nephilim consulted amongst themselves until they were of one accord. For all of their indoctrinations, the ANCs knew that they were witnessing the closest thing to what they themselves felt like clamped down into in the Empyrean. Dim thoughts of gratitude for how they'd been paired effectively rose.

"The next time they flicker to happy-meal range, we all pounce, pull them apart...and Puryf them as unique, in and of-"

"But won't that-"an ANC countered before the two within it realized they had no clue what the separation would do.

"What about Sector-system?" another one asked.
"Sector will record that the half-life was processed. How is never specified in the protocol-"

"Go!" another ANC yelled as their opportunity as the aspects flickered down to child size. The ANCs swarmed the two thrashing boys and roughly yanked them apart instead of shoving them back together again as initially ordered.

They processed them one at a time separated by a few other beings also being calibrated for reentry into the upper realms.

At the end of the calibration, the ANCs warily turned the two boys towards each other around a patch of construct that would grow with the one placed within it. The ANCs flinched as the two leaned towards one another then stopped, glaring at each other in confusion. Slowly the white construct below them pulled itself into three patches before it all evaporated in front of the ANCs eyes.

"Anad-" only one boy looked up at the start of the halflife's name being said, face scowled with curse words that never would sound the same to him again. His hair frothed atop his head like a chia pet and pulsed with his insolence.

"Look-Wait-watch-" the ANC murmured then said "Hezuz!" The head of the one whose hair suddenly spooled out like ringlets of black silk ribbon ringlets sneered then flashed the most despotic grin any of the Nephilim present had ever seen. They took it in, collectively shocked.

"What now?" an ANC whispered.
"Opposite ends of the spectrum?" another suggested.

All present agreed. One of the boys possessed an angular defiance that was so intense that it would make sense under only one watch. The one called Anad was transcribed and reentered the earthly realm in the joy division, under the cloaked dominion of Third Head of Council.

But the one who had looked up to the name of Hezuz, something about his child-like yet sneering royal diffidence spoke volumes about the futility of placing him within the ranks of First or Second Council without all hell breaking loose. The ANCs looked to the boy and then at one another, then towards the boy again, who sighed like he was a weary monarch and they were trying his patience.

"The Anannke-" the ANCs all said in unison. And it was done.

chapter twelve

"Make it go away-" she whispered determinedly.

The chaos of an unplanned family reunion swirled around the child in front of the mirror in her grandfather's room as she looked into it but not really. Uncle after Aunt peered in suspiciously, all but one ready to hurl a loud insult her way in case she was admiring herself. Nip it in the bud while they're young was the way things went around here, unconsciously or not.

"What do you think you're do- " the sentence began again and again, somehow always catching in their throats, due to them all subconsciously remembering that this was the room their father had consciously killed their mother in over the years with one cruel sentence after another. This broken look would coat their faces before they shuffled away and left her alone to stare off into space. It was the only room within that house that Anukai felt safe in.

She sat there folded into herself, staring off into the mirror in boyish little clothes. Cords and a button-down cowboy shirt with actual horses embroidered on the yokes, in the middle of summer, buttoned up wrong. Her face was washed. She said it again.

"Make it go away-"

"What? Make what go away?" The invisible little boy she could see next to her in her reflection whispered back absently through his own mirror a thousand miles away, his dirty Spiderman underoos tee pulled up over his head as he tried to work up the nerve to look down at the slowly healing skin

knotted across his little bird chest. Something pregnant in the pause made him look up.

He tilted his head to the side so the little wild-haired girl popped into focus. Her long ponytails were encased with what looked like a month's worth of lint and fuzz that was probably only a weeks, but somehow due to the internal flare, her visuals read to him how the feelings of not being cared for registered to her.

"What is-What's wrong?" He stuttered hoarsely. His voice danced across the surface of her like a breeze able to push things away. "May-make what go away?!" He asked again, his voice climbing quickly up an octave to the fever-pitched wail of the panic attack slamming into him that she was too numb to hear.

"The smell-" she groaned softly."-The smell-" she whispered again, then cut the connect between suddenly.

chapter thirteen

From across the hall, The Tsunga of the family could see the tip of the little kid's shoe. Her lips curled up into an insane, self-satisfied snarl. *"Go make her do it again with everybody here- shove her into it- but in His room-"* something on her seethed into her inner ear. The Tsunga was eighteen. She started to walk across the hall.

"Do it!" The things inside of her leered, egging her on. *"We already took this house- She thinks she's safe....in there?! Hahahaha-"* The legions inside the head of the malevolent woman-child cackled so loud that they were the only things real to her, the only things that had ever been 'there' for her, them, and the things they told her to do. *"She's not safe in there! That's where we got to you!"*

The little kid curled up tighter on top of the dresser holding her breath, defiant and terrified. She heard everything the demons said to the Tsunga. Out of nowhere, Anukai's favorite aunt Corinth cut across the Tsunga's path, snapping the demons out of twisted revelries.

"Watch where you goin!" Corinth roared like the Amazon she was, shaking the things latched into The Tsunga so badly that it showed on the younger aunt's face. Corinth went outside where the party was. Just as quickly, The Tsunga shook it off and was back on course, face twisted up like a bully, oblivious to the fact that something had made Corinth turn around and watch her through the mesh screen.

Before the Tsunga could take another step, the little kid exploded into action, violent tears streaming down her face in rage as she flew into the bathroom, slammed the door and locked it, turning on the sink and shower faucets as well as the old radio, cranking it up to drown out what she knew was to come next. Even though she'd heard the door latch, something inside the Tsunga still made her try the doorknob.

"Aww... you crybaby-" she hissed, face against the door, looking over her shoulder to make sure no one else heard. "Don't cry for it, baby" the Tsunga laughed. "Maybe later-" she cackled crazily, everything inside her howling along with her. She pressed her body against the length of the door, aroused by the fear she imagined the little kid to be reeling from and the fear she herself remembered from long ago. The fear she'd conquered by doing to her nieces and nephews what had been done to her. Eyes rolled back in the Tsunga's head as she imagined stealing even more of what had been stolen from her so long ago.

The Tsunga got off as much as she had when she first grabbed the special little "firstborn grandchild" by her throat and rammed her face into her crotch that hadn't been washed since the last time her brother-in-law had attacked her in the basement, literally right under the porch her own father was passed-out drunk on.

Anukai took the bar of safeguard soap that was melted on the sink into her hands and lathered, blanked out by the silent rage inside of her.

"I know! I'll offer to *baby-sit* yall! Then-no interruptions- you'd like that, wouldn't you?!" the Tsunga snarled softly, wetting her lips as she pressed them against the door and jiggled the knob again.

"You gotta tell someone-" the little kid said to herself.

"We already told, remember?! And Daddy beat us- "

"Then you tell someone else- that's what they say to do-tell until-"

*"Why? Daddy already told our teacher we were a liar- "*she cried softly.

"Who else?! The Mother?! She knows! She doesn't care!"

"SHUT-up, stop talking about it!" she whispered harshly to herself as she washed her hands again and again, the conversation shooting from eye to eye.

Heat wave's always and forever danced in the air thanks to WZAK. Tears began to spill down her face. She washed her face raw, jamming gooey chunks of soap into her eyes, refusing to scream, demanding the tears to stop, that she numb out again.

"It doesn't matter- we gotta tell somebody else!" She gasped. *"We gotta do something-find somebody else- I can't - They call us a liar and still have her watch us! We gotta tell somebody else! We have to do something!"* She couldn't even mouth shut up anymore. She just re lathered. And washed it all away in the gap. *"I'm...clean. I'm...clean. I'm...clean. I'm...clean. I'm... clean. I'm...clean. I'm...clean. I'm...clean. I'm...clean. I'm.. .clean. I'm...clean. I'm...clean. I'm...clean. I'm...clean. I'm.. .clean. I'm...clean. I'm...clean. I'm...clean. I'm...clean. I'm.. .clean. I'm...clean. I'm...clean. I'm...clean."* The little kid chanted inside of herself without moving her lips for what seemed like an eternity.

Then she remembered something that didn't make any sense, but made all the sense in the world. Her heart reminded her that "She" wasn't even really "from here" anyway.

That she had been where she was from a long time ago.. .before he had vanished at the foot of her bed.

Out of nowhere, the invisible little boy crept up behind her in the mirror, shaking as he nervously wrapped his scarred arms around her and hugged her, knowing she couldn't feel him, but that eventually she'd see he was there.

"Hi~" the boy whispered in her ear. Her head tilted to the side. The blank look on her face melted into recognition. Her rigid little body softened a bit. Slowly he eased the sticky remnants of the safeguard out of her grip. "Stop washing your face."

Her eyes were red, raw from the chemicals in the soap. Her face had been washed until it was too tender to touch without her realizing the smell of her unwashed aunt was in her dirty hair that her mother hated to deal with.

Suddenly the Tsunga banged roughly on the door. "WHAT are you doing in there!?!" The Tsunga screamed, showing out as if she'd been waiting to use the bathroom under the sudden hawk-like glare of her own father who'd slid into the kitchen from out back and had seen the Tsunga all but grinding onto the doorjamb.

Out of nowhere, the little kid threw her entire body up against the door so violently that its hinges shook. The Tsunga jumped back in shock, whirled around and ran out the side door, straight into a glaring Corinth, who was heading back into the house to see what the Tsunga was actually up to. Tsunga cursed upon seeing the look in Corinth's eye and took off down the driveway to her friend's house.

The little girl laughed uncontrollably as she relaxed back into the little boy's arms. Her eyes would've filled up with tears of joy if not burned dry by the soap.

The boy stepped around her and laid his faded scalp against her forehead before standing up a bit straighter, his face resting on her unkempt hair. He sniffed absently and recoiled. "What's that in your hair?" he croaked softly.

Anukai yanked herself away from him and looked at him as if she'd been slapped, confused. The comprehension slammed into her head like lightning. She crumpled as if she'd been stabbed and looked up at him, wounded. Hyperventilating against the dirty tub she angrily slammed her face into it, howling. "Stupid! Stupid! Stupid!"

"Holy shi-Shi-" He began to stutter, "No! No- it's not your hair- it's in your hair-stop it! Stop it!!!" He screamed, verging on hyperventilating himself. He pulled her away from the tub in the mirror. She slashed at the empty air around her.

"Don't touch me! Don't YOU touch me!!"She screamed in the mirror. Her voice boomed inside of his head in his house, while in her bathroom, all was silent.

"Stop it!!!" he squealed as she fought him off and slammed her head into the coil at the base of the toilet, ripping skin off of her forehead on the exposed nail. Although two years older than her in the spirit, he was only a little taller and did his best to pin and then pull her into the far corner as she bit into his hand that tried to cover her mouth, holding her tightly. In the mirror blood was everywhere, even splattered across it.

"Don't worry-" He whispered as she cried. "Don't-worry- I'll wash your hair in here- so you won't get into trouble. I'll wash your hair in here."

chapter fourteen

They had all gathered in the vestibule. Windows the size of ships cut into giant slabs of polished stone looked down onto the Empyrean from the throne-room of the Anannke's Purification complex, glistening like dream-catchers, the snare of each eye woven together from strands of twisted silk that resembled spider webs. Studded black leather chaises were scattered on wooden lanai that snaked along the perimeter of the wide- open receiving space, pushed up against low-lying tables with brightly burning braziers in their centers. Above, carved teak beams were draped with white fibers and red, blue and green prayer flags. Red sky pressed against the bruised glass that enclosed the space. The throne room sparkled due to the molten gold and copper pool the decks were built upon. The area towards the center of the large space was conspicuously empty, with another large eye woven into the glass directly above it. Clusters of itinerant nobles temporarily at court gingerly strolled about in platform sandals made of carved wood that clunked along the decks. The click-clack of wood on wood blended into the sounds that poured forth from solitary musicians placed on pedestals scattered across the lanai while they plucked at divine instruments. The competing solos fused into melodies and cavorted with the other sounds that danced across the space to the delight of those present, recently perfected beings who practiced their freshly purified rituals of reserve, reverence and murmured worship with one another.

Alongside the polished decks, domesticated tigers ambled about. They occasionally sprawled or defecated atop open grates in the floor above trenches. Multi-lingual mantras, chanting, and twisted Negro spirituals that embraced climbing up the rough sides of mountains poured out of them, the wails punctuated by sobs and the tingling of tambourines as once-called gurus, church mothers and spiritual fathers sat in tight, rigid rows below-ground, forcibly swaddled in the orange set aside for monks from the hips down. They cried out to the celebrated Spiritual Beings of yore to *Hare*, Hurry forth for salvation, even though they no longer answered calls above or below due to the atrocities such humans had consciously committed in their names. They cried in the name of a God they had sold and profited due to but had never taken the time to truly know and do the true work of. Charlatans were purged by the continual impact of tiger dung and discarded aromatic tea by the nobles as it sloshed through the grates and scalded the perpetrating holy men and women now tightly confined within sewers of the purifying section of the highest heaven.

Faithless, they howled in hopes that they could be saved by anything that looked like works in spite of all they'd systematically devoured in those strong enough to believe but too weak to sincerely see the content of the character of those they followed down on Earth. The titles of deities tumbled chaotically, in tongues. Those who had followed a God of Peace yet encouraged millions to kill in the name of It had long ago given up faith in him ever showing up, and instead co-opted as many names of foreign gods cried out to alongside them as they could pronounce.

Frauds who had sounded spiritual battle-cries on Earth with no sense of reprisal sang out in horror across false religions in ways that were almost poetic to the nobles who lolled about above, ascended beings who had once been ensnared by the mind-grips of gurus then impoverished, beings strong enough at death due to meekness in life to plead their case at crossing and demand the seven-fold remuneration upon entry into the afterlife they'd been promised. They got their versions of it simply because they knew enough to ask. They enjoyed the unspoken inverted caste system to the hilt as they lounged over the heads of those who'd once used their faith against them.

The courtiers and courtesans were now visibly perfected, and the scars once caused by fatal leaps of hope based on misinformation were no longer visible. The sound of all the stolen spirit songs spun together deliciously inside the reception hall, like a supernatural riff on rhythm and blues.

The Anannke sat enthroned on a pile of indigo silk pillows off to the side of one of the circular windows alone. The strands of her white hair lazily looped up overhead to create her own curtains of state across the banners of red, blue and green that separated aristocratic cliques. Hair dangled from the exposed rafters above her and crawled out into the palace around her. With it she was absently tuned into every heartbeat within the confines of Puryf if she wanted to be, as well as throughout the Empyrean and Earth. Every cloaked thought, desire, and urge that the recently ascended beings buried inside of themselves was on offer to her if she so pleased.

All attempts by the nobles at being presentable and perhaps prized by Fate during the pomp and circumstance of purified court-life were simply wasted effort. They did their best to come off as cleaner than any of them needed to be in order to deserve the impending experience of Heaven, let alone could ever be since it was all secretly about a gift of grace anyway. This fallacy in their thought life was indicated by their presence in this particular purification citadel but they refused to leave until they were perfect in their own eyes. They were only concerned with how it all looked on the outside, which set them all up to always find something that could be a little less askew. So for the most part this batch would never leave and she knew it. So she tolerated them. Almost like family.

Out of boredom with those who had chosen to linger on, she seemingly remained quiet. No one at court had any memories of the sound of the Anannke, though there were rumors that those beings who actually survived Puryf to finally enter the Empyrean had the echo of her blessing as the last thing they heard before being drained down. What the Nobles addicted to the atmosphere of Puryf didn't realize was that she spoke around them continuously, even if only to entertain herself with the sounds of their screams.

The consciously cruel treble in her voice was so intense that unless she was very careful the sound of her speaking simply exploded all the synapses within their heads and blanked them out, making residual blood they'd thought they'd been hiding painfully run out of their ears as her vibration pulled them closer towards the pointless perfection they so craved. The aristocrats of the zone had been striving for the summit of so-called flawlessness for so long that they averted their eyes from the most pure of them all in order to stay sane and stay put, satisfied with their own false senses of progress. The Anannke had been beyond the minute concept of perfection for so long that even to gaze upon her caused bouts of shame within them.

On the other side of the huge hall, Hezuz, the obscenely beautiful little splintered-off boy with skin the color of sandpaper, was the only one mortified enough by her beauty to surreptitiously study the Crone whose name no one at court dared to call. He was the one that was whispered must be hers and would one day be perfect enough to be King of Kings.

She had been basking in the red light of the sky for so long that she'd since forgotten what had first brought her to her knees. As she worked her mystery absently, his courage grew. His eyes slowly slid up from the glistening feet of the Anannke. Yard upon yard of precisely pleated sheer white fabric undulated around her. Gold, bronze and silver details of cranes feasting on snakes were embroidered across her back, along the edges of her elongated cuffs and the eventual outskirts of her hem. The pleated outyr garment cut away to reveal a honey-coated and gold-dusted decolletage, thrust out for all to see if they dared to look. Her blatantly exposed undyr was a delicate sheath made of metallic chain-mail mesh that descended from the edges of her areole's to her gold and copper dipped toes. The Anannke was the only one who dared to be barefoot in the vestibule.

She was completely aware of the half-life boy Hezuz as she dangled random strands of hair in front of herself like the strings of a harp in a drawn-out fashion. The fingers of her lowered right hand discreetly trailed across the surface of the liquid gold floor and then returned to the rhythm woven by the left. She consciously flicked them so that the glint of her gold finger tips refracted and hit Hezuz in the eye, making him stir in a manner that drew unwanted attention from those around him.

The little girls trained to clam our to fulfill his every need and pine for his presence jumped into action. They rose up and surrounded him with queries as to all the things he might possibly like them to immediately do. Their blank eyes flashed against one another as they tried to quietly jostle for his attention and eventual affection without touching, thoughts centered on visions of being alongside him in the Empyrean once he made his ascension to the throne that those who cultivated them continually whispered about as the little girls sat stoically in stasis. The desire was born anew at every rise. All clamored to be *Eloh* to his eventually adult, and crown worthy *'im*.

He glared against the sudden unwarranted assistance, knowing that it had nothing to do with the truth of him at all. "You want to do something for me?" He hissed, eyes flashing as his face twisted up. "Get these!" the evil beautiful boy snarled and threw his carved sandals barely over their heads into the wet gold of the floor behind them. The beautiful bevy looked away and sat again, pinned in place, collectively downcast.

His huge sloe-like eyes danced back towards the masterful weave-working of the Anannke under the shield of heavily fringed lashes and a wild mass of ribbon-like curls that he'd tousled forth to hide behind. The eyes of the Anannke never acknowledged him, but he swore he saw a faint smile play across the corner of her lips. He flashed his eyes at her and defiantly refused to look away again.

He noticed there was a gentle, yet cold and calculated methodology to her movements. The only strands that ever seemed to be truly tangled were blackened ones that danced around from the nape of her somewhat exposed neck. And the knots were ripped out ruthlessly.

Knots that happened among the more wizened strands were given the kid glove treatment. The Anannke peered at each strand forever as different emotions crossed her face like storm clouds and sun showers, almost out of her control.

Occasionally, the little golden blades that spun at the inside-center of her wrists would snip through a strand of hair below her line of sight, the disconnected strand momentarily caught up in the shock of the blade right before it disintegrated into smoke. At other times, the Anannke would remove various-sized pairs of fragile looking golden scissors from the rim of her outermost obi and snip at the silver-white hairs, feathering a strand here and there gingerly, as if giving birth to a new brood of babies at every turn. Seldom did any two strands that she gently plaited seem to stay twisted together for long.

"Don't flinch~" the Anannke murmured out of nowhere and chuckled.

chapter fifteen

Anukai had been huddled in the tub for so long that she couldn't feel her legs anymore. She had watched the sun travel from east to west on her knees as the little boy did what he could, lathering her up with head and shoulders shampoo he'd found under his own sink in his grandmother's bathroom on the other side of the mirror. She had even fallen asleep, at which point he took the time to wash blood from his friend's face then gently rub lotion from her grand-dad's cabinet into her cheeks. He had even bent down and gingerly kissed the little girl on her forehead where the cut from slamming her head into the toilet was, and watched in awe as the skin unfurled around the impact of his lips and healed itself right then and there. Her cheek was salty and sticky where blood and tears that had finally found a way out had dried like her now shampooed and rebraided hair. Sun poured in through the frosted window thrown slightly open to the sounds of the going-away barbeque in the backyard. He was shocked and pleased with how it turned out, and woke her to take a look for herself.

A beautiful lopsided French braid ran diagonally down the back of her head. Little tendrils he couldn't get to stay in it spun wildly down the sides of her face. He blushed hotly and looked at his toes as she danced her fingertips over the prettiest hairstyle she had ever been given in her life, and said as much. To him her eyes looked as if she were about to burst out into song when her hand flew up to her forehead and discovered the cut wasn't just healed in the mirror.

"Anukai..." her aunt Corinth whispered from the other side of the door for the third time. Anukai's head whipped round to it, then back to the little boy. It was the first time the little girl had heard her.

Her hand flew up to his face and gently pressed into it as his did the same to hers, a weird whispered thanks to one another before fading from each other's sight. And just like that, she was alone in the bathroom, hearing the aunt that was going away gingerly calling out to her in the hallway. She shyly opened the door and stood face to face with a kneeling Amazon she called Queen in her head.

"Doing your hair?" her favorite aunt murmured, watching her like a cat. Anukai shrugged her shoulders then jumped as one of the doors slammed shut somewhere in the house. "She's not back yet." She said softly to the little girl who looked away. "You know who I mean when I say that, right?" Anukai nodded, still unable to look at Corinth, words inside her little head telling her it was pointless to tell anybody else again as other words screamed at her that now was her chance.

"Come here-" Corinth reached out to Anukai and the little girl flinched as she took hold. "Look at me, Anukai," her aunt cooed in the odd, gravelly way she used to when Anukai was a baby, the way that weirded everybody else out, but had calmed the child down like she was hearing God himself. Corinth was so done with the drama in her father's house that as soon as she got "saved," her first order of business had been to find a way to move as far away from the madness and as close to Christ as she could possibly get. She was leaving after the party. Anukai looked up and tears fell from horrified eyes that pleaded with her to not make her tell. "Why did you wash your hair, Anukai?"

The little girl started to say she didn't, an angel did, then paused, because the little boy wasn't really an angel, and she wondered if Corinth believed in angels as strongly as she did in the God she was now following down to Alabama to the shock of everyone.

"To wash the smell of her out of it." The words fell out of the little girl's mouth so plainly that for a moment even she didn't even realize what she had said.

"What did she-" her aunt stopped as the full extent of what Anukai said hit her in the face like a brick. Her aunt hissed harshly, scaring the little girl, who tried to get away.

"No, no-" her aunt cried out softly and grabbed her into a bear-hug. "Not mad at you- not you, Anukai-why didn't you-" she whispered.

"I did, but daddy whipped me for telling and said I was lying, even told my teachers I was a liar 'just in case' before I said anything to anyone else-" Anukai cried out, stunned by Corinth's shaking. "and my mama don't care-"

"Where-?" Corinth asked woodenly. Anukai pointed to the room that had been Corinth's before she'd moved out. "Almost every time she baby-sits us--she makes me- and today she threatened to do it even with yall here-" Anukai wheezed in her throat.

"Come on-" Corinth said abruptly and angrily stood up, Anukai in hand as they walked over to the door. She felt the shudder pass through the child as she turned the knob.

Anukai looked up at her aunt and they walked in together. Corinth went to both windows in the bedroom and the tiny unheard of window in the closet and threw them open to let the funk of the room air out. She remembered the first time she had found Anukai camped out in the closet playing with her dolls-it had been her favorite place in the whole house. The little girl called it her room, said it was a room because it had a window, and they had all gotten tired of arguing with her about it.

"I was playing in my room. making a movie with my dolls. Then she-" Anukai startled as the Tsunga loudly came back up the driveway. The hackles on the back of both the child and her other aunt raised up.

"Stay here-" Corinth hissed.

"But-" Anukai started.
"I said stay here—go to the window in your room-" Corinth barked and shot out the bedroom.

Anukai trembled as she ran into the closet, slammed the door behind her. She clumsily knocked over stuff to get up into the window and looked out as Corinth's first slap made contact with the side of the Tsunga's face, knocking her back down the driveway into the full view of everybody on the street. A scream of shock stuck in the little girl's throat as half the family ran from the backyard while Corinth beat the snot out of Tsunga, calling her all the names that the Tsunga had called the little girl.

"I know what you did! I know what you're doing! It's NOT Her fault! What happened to YOU is not Anukai's fault! You disgusting bitch!" She slapped and kicked at her younger sister as their siblings tried to pull her off.

"YOU fucking Beast!" she roared. Every time their siblings would get Corinth off of Tsunga, she would have something smart to say and Corinth would break free and wail on her again. Older brothers ran for cover because she was equal-opportunity when she went off.

The little girl tried not to howl as her heart soared and sliced through the air in time with the punches of Corinth into the Tsunga, elated.

"Stop it, Corinth! You're gonna Kill her!" brothers yelled as the older sisters charged the fight to pull the two youngest sisters apart.

"Stop?! Do you know what she did?!-See! You're protecting her?!! This is why I'm Outta here!" Corinth yelled as they coddled the bloodied youngest sister. "Tell them what you did! Tell them!" Corinth screamed.

"Nothing- i didn't-" Tsunga spat.
Corinth slammed through the protective arms of her older sisters like they weren't even there and violently bashed her younger sister's face in. "You Liar! You disgusting cunt! Liar! How dare you!" Corinth screamed as the whole street gathered to watch the spectacle. No one had seen Corinth go off like that since she had discovered God a few years earlier, and all present swore she's kill Tsunga if God himself didn't intervene.

Just then, cars rolled up. The new spiritual sisters and brothers of Corinth jumped out, praying in tongues under their breaths, sending many of the onlookers fleeing from the cloud of spirit that rose up to have Corinth's back. The demons that ran rough-shod all over the house they were there to deliver Corinth from hurled insults at the bible thumpers.

"Just go, Corinth- we'll handle this- just go-" The eldest sister whispered, her eyes darting between the hushed prayers of the cult that had already brainwashed Corinth into leaving her family and a shocked Anukai watching it all from Tsunga's closet.

"But-" Corinth started vehemently.
"I promise you," the eldest sister said evenly," we. Will. handle. it. You? You...go...with ...god."
Corinth looked back at her new spiritual family.

The blue black man called Ebon barely nodded his head and the rest of them climbed back into their sedans to wait for her. Banyan, the pitch-black one heading south for the first time alongside Corinth popped open a parasol of worn kente cloth scraps pieced together and encrusted with beads and shells. Banyan's nervous smile ignited a completely different fire in the chest of Corinth and she stormed into the house to grab her suitcases. Anukai ploughed right into her, face wet with tears of gratitude.

"Come on," Corinth whispered and pulled Anukai into the bathroom with her so both of them could wash the rage tears off their faces as her older siblings dragged the Tsunga into the backyard to rinse the blood off of her in silence.

"She's sick, Anukai." Corinth muttered. "All of them are since mama, but maybe even before. But this is not your fault. You did nothing wrong. No matter what happens next, remember that, ok?"

She grabbed the little girl's chin and steadied her. The sparks shooting from Corinth's Hazel eyes landed with soft thuds against Anukai's retinas. They seeped in and pushed already cracked scales all the way out of them. Anukai's chest shook. "Remember that, okay? And you should have never been hit for telling what she did." Anukai nodded and the two of them blushed at each other before splashing their faces with cold water again.

"...Are you really...going with God?" Anukai asked Corinth softly as she watched the shards of scales wash down the drain. Her head was clear of anger and fear for the first time in the super long eight years of her life.

Corinth paused. "Yeah, I guess so," she whispered back, as a slow smile pushed across her face. "He lives in me, said it's time for a move...so I'm going with him," she laughed softly, then turned red as Banyan flashed across her mind.

"Are you gonna get in trouble with God for hitting Tsunga for me?" Anukai asked warily.

"Nah-Who do you think exploded out of me when you told me? There's this scripture- in the bible- says something like "Better for a man to be dropped in the ocean with a big rock round his neck than for God to get hold of him for hurting his kids.""

Corinth smiled as Anukai looked at her doubtfully. "And you don't know it yet, Anukai, but you one of his kids. My big brother shoulda beat Her ass, not yours for telling. But like I said, they're all still sick over mama right now, letting all kinds of mess go down- and everything else-"

"I don't want you to go." Anukai whispered harshly.

"You just remember that you can too -when you get old enough. No matter what they tell you. If they don't get better, you can leave too. I love you Anukai." Corinth hugged her as her church family tooted the horn for her outside.

"I love you too. And Thank You-" Anukai whispered. They walked out the bathroom hand in hand.

Anukai struggled to help Corinth drag one of her suitcases through the house to the porch where her drunk grandfather had slept through the entire battle. Ebon and Banyan ran up, grabbed the suitcases from the two of them and put them in the trunk of the car.

Corinth walked over to her passed-out father and looked up at the sky like she was debating with God about something. She bent down and woodenly hugged her dad, gingerly placing a kiss on his gin-soaked cheek. He stirred a little, cussed, then fell back into his stupor.

Corinth hugged Anukai one last time as the little girl silently crumbled down on the steps as aunts and uncles all stiffly hugged their second to littlest sister goodbye.

Ebon held open the backdoor in the lead sedan for her. Anukai watched as Banyan opened back up the big, colorful umbrella and twirled it a bit in the grip of his hand, making the shells and beads jingle nervously.

Corinth locked eyes with Banyan and all sound stopped as Anukai watched this sheepish, shy grin break out in a blast of white from the man's face as the sparks from her aunt's eyes sunk into him like they had done to her in the bathroom. Suddenly, the sound of the bells was the only thing Anukai heard. She didn't know why, but she felt like the dark man had made that umbrella, just for her aunt, just for that day.

Her jaw dropped as little pink flowers floated silently in the air around Banyan and Corinth, as if caught up in a vortex of energy between them. Corinth looked back over her shoulder one last time at Anukai, eyes still shooting sparks all over the place, making sure the little girl saw what she had no real way of understanding yet, then ducked into the car, Banyan right behind her. Ebon walked around to the driver's side and got in. Corinth and Banyan waved at Anukai, grinning at the eight year old as the tinted window rolled up and the car pulled off.

Soon as the car containing Corinth turned the corner, all of Anukai's aunts and uncles came up and crowded around her then shuffled away one at a time, not one of them bringing up the blood stains being washed down the driveway to the sewer or anything else that had led to the fireworks at the end of Corinth's goodbye party.

They left the little girl out on the porch alone with their passed-out father, who watched the sun turn the sky red as she encouraged herself anyway.

"Somebody cared. Corinth cared. Forget the rest of'em. Corinth...cared." Anukai muttered as the pink flowers followed the setting sun over the horizon.

chapter sixteen

The little boy named Gabryl sat at the top of what used to be his mother's bed in the dark, his whole body curled up in a ball in the corner. He was silent, his face ashy from crying all the way there, pressed against the coolness of the wall in an attempt to calm himself down because no one else could. They didn't know he could hear every word uttered in the other room.

"Danise, what are you going to do?" His grandmother snapped sternly at his mother. "I know you're hurting, child, but you have two sons left in the wake of this that need you to be strong-"

"Mama, I don't know what to do-" Danise sighed. "You know how to do everything right- why don't you tell me what to do with my kids!" she snapped.

"Child- this isn't about you! It isn't even about that man of yours who went and got himself killed- and almost took your son with him!"

"It isn't ever about me, Mama! When is it going to be about me?" Danise whined like the teenager she never got to be and hadn't legally been in a very long time.

"Danise!" Her mother snapped, "I had to go pick that boy up from school- Again- Because they couldn't find you! Because he got into a fight and almost took another boy's eye out- over all this stuff that you keep acting like didn't happen-"

"He Doesn't' talk to me either, Mama! What am I supposed to do?" She hissed. "He ain't been right since before his- He don't talk to me either-"

"Shut up and Listen Danise! He doesn't talk because you won't shut up with your spoiled woe is me act long enough to even try to help him! He already knows you have written him off as "not right!" Why should he talk to you!" His grandmother yelled as she prayed-*Lord, please help me to get through to this child you blessed me with*! The grandmother took a deep breath.

"Do realize that in the entire time you've been here, you have not even thought to ask why he got into the fight?" Danise opened her mouth to angrily interject but the look that darkened her mother's face silenced her. "All his classmates know. The twisted teachers told them, used him as an example of what happens to bad little boys who take candy from strangers! And some sick little boy, with a few other nasty little boys egging him on, tried to touch him in the bathroom. And when he shoved him off, the other ones who had stood there watching this bigger kid try to molest him, they tried to grab him, wanting to see the scars-And he-"

The grandmother's voice shook. "He got away from the boys and the ringleader cried out "You're just crazy! Just like your little brother! And you liked it! My big brother said it only happens to kids who like it-And that's why your father died! Cause he knew what was wrong with you! He wanted to get away from you-!"

"The boys told the Principal Gabryl's face went blank and he went for the nasty little boy's eyes, screaming "Stop Seeing that!" as he...ripped open the kid's face- so could get to-whatever Gabryl thinks was making him say-" Tears started to roll down his grandmother's cheeks at the same time they broke silently out of Gabryl against the wall in the other room.

Her daughter stood mute as she watched her own mother try to gain back composure. "I...I can't do this momma-"Danise whispered as she backed away towards the door. " I- I can't-"

"Danise, he needs his mother!" His grandmother sighed as her daughter ploughed out the door in search of a fix.

The boy's breath hitched in his throat as he heard the latch on the door click with his mother on the outside. He couldn't cry anymore. He already knew that she saw the same thing that Jarvis yelled in the bathroom fight because she had said it all to him when she was high, repeatedly.

Said it was his fault, that he ruined everything. The scars on his chest started to itch. The pressure of the howl trapped in him echoed in his ears until the water in his head broke and he whispered up towards the ceiling. *Please God-I know you don't love me- but just please let me sleep- let me sleep.*

chapter seventeen

The feet of Comptroller Yris barely touched the streets of gold after her session with Sr. Vayo Kahn Diaz. Her head remained flooded with all she knew about the beyond untouchable, above and below board.

While under charge to construct a Xanadu-like decompression zone to balance the training construct aspect of Puryf that was to help others like himself not adjusting to the somatic atmosphere of elevated life as easily without the council admitting there was a problem, the one called Vayo Kahn stumbled upon fault lines in the Empyrean to a tangible place that, by all Tryage rhetoric to the contrary, could not exist in a physical sense any longer.

The experience of the truth created a blip in Diaz's system to accommodate the swallowing of the daily lie that the waves were reaching them from a distant past, a point in time that had already destroyed itself and had no impact on them in the eternal reality of the Empyrean outside of studying the concepts of Comptrolling and Spiritual Guardianship in various constructs.

According to the Tryage, the Denizens "treated" in the D/o theatre were doing nothing more than the ancient pastime of addictively watching repeat broadcasts of dead people unable to get into a heaven that didn't make sense once you struck below the surface. Reels on repeat of those who'd ended up in Hell instead of Heaven after the end of the world, supposedly to remind them how lucky they were.

Vayo Kahn's mainframe had taken to sporadically going spiritually suicidal, shutting down into a kamikaze jump to who knows where. Each jump was blanked from his memory upon his recapture by force during the compulsory no-holds barred purification process executed prior to official entry into the Empyrean.

The fumes that rose up from the fault line Diaz built upon flowed freely through the hive-like ocular memorial pleasure dome he designed, and also had the tendency to temporarily expose the lie of "no escape" to those who ended up in the Demi-ourgos (complex-D/o) Amphitheatre- a truth the Denizens got silently addicted to like a drug. The same suicidal jumping the shark that continually sprung Diaz in a way that the Tryage was not ready to deal with beyond making proof of it repeatedly go away began to gnaw at the Others routinely in attendance, unbeknownst to them. Their inability to truly touch one another blocked the connect or the report.

Those unable to swallow the lie even as they lived it, yet rewired to not speak out against it were sneeringly called Denizens by the Citizens of the Empyrean. Dissatisfaction with the reality of "Heaven" seemed to shine out of their skins, their existence an unveiled accusation against those shallow enough to accept the feed that the Tryage sent out. For a Citizen strung out instead on the fragile bliss of Heavenly Ever After keyed into how hollow their interpretation and pursuit of initial life had been, to cross paths with a Denizen on the streets of gold was like a black woman sitting at a white counter during Jim Crow, too fleshy to embrace the joys of finally being elevated to heavenly noble untouchable status.

Denizens hid from the red light like rats, pooled around the Ancient Ruins on the outskirts of the Empyrean.Citizens that had all their material wishes granted as long as one didn't delve too deep, never dug.

But in the complex constructed by Vayo Kahn, many Denizens trapped into the pantomime of day-tripping their best afterlife yet came out after the closest thing to dark they had patched into those they somehow knew were not phantoms of a past but instead still alive and left behind below.

Many tried to carry on the Citizen sham of elevated spiritual existence, above the need to connect, or be held, but after the first hyperrealistic toke of the holograms Diaz's fire in the hole tapped, it was only a matter of time. They too crumbled inside themselves and looked in on Earth with longing, praying that there really was something higher than the Tryage that ruled a red-taped highest high in the Empyrean that this true God heard them, and would somehow set them free. Scores of Denizens went missing in the wake of Vayo Kahn's falls, his absence a covert alarm to others about to combust that a window of sorts was somehow open, with no time to lose. They plummeted in disconnected droves, unaware they were not alone, dropping down to an Earth that Empyrean mandate proclaimed no longer even existed.

The bureaucracy of the Tryage acted as if no such absenteeism could ever occur, to the mortification of those left alone in the wake of the jumper. With no recognition of a problem in Heaven, a lone Denizen unable to discover the whereabouts of his partner went mad from his pain panic, and this silent sense of ignored loss. He put the face of his friend on the side of a carton of milk he couldn't drink and waited. When he could wait no more, he submitted his own photo, and was never seen in the Empyrean again.

"But why was I even assigned to this? And what is the problem if they really aren't going anywhere outside of constructs? If the past is over and there is nothing to go back to?" the

Comptroller thought aloud to herself. Suddenly a word crested in the sea of her subconscious.

Anadhezuz

"Stop it." Comptroller Yris muttered to herself as her energy cut its way through the crowd ahead of her. It was the name of the half-lifer Sr. Vayo Kahn Diaz always referred to as H.G. Wails hung in the spaces between her thoughts as if her cell walls were constructed from the syllables.

Anadhezuz.

There was no place for her to hide from the echo of it as she wandered aimlessly through the canyons of the Empyrean. As soon as she pushed it out of her head enough to focus on a face or texture around her it pounced again, as the swoosh of black crows playing mating games echoed overhead, no shadow in any direction whenever she looked down.

Anadhezuz.

Exasperated, she stopped in front of a glass structure that swooped up the side of the canyon like an elaborate aria, sprawling poetically, swelling with the promise of what this level of life was purported to be. Comptroller Yris just stood there. Dead. Looking for her reflection and seeing nothing at first. Then a woman, somewhere other than where the Comptroller was now, full of beauty, promise and this strange darkness that weighed most of the light in her eyes down towards her belly, causing Yris to look down at the woman's stomach too, just in time to see the life still left in her bleed out of the reflection's belly. When Yris looked back up she was face to face with a haggard, beautiful old woman looking back at her, greying at the temples with every breath, daring the Comptroller to deny her existence.

Horrified, Yris turned and stumbled through the citizens of the Empyrean realm towards D/o theatre.

chapter eighteen

The empty bottles had been arranged methodically in a meadow of glass that filled the entire backyard. There were red bottles for the rose garden, discarded Heinekens created the sun- soaked glens of green, and wine bottles built out the shadows. They represented pools of water and every other flower he couldn't bring to his inebriated mind as he peered over his shoulder from on his back upon the roof of the old row house.

He rolled over in a stupor, burning himself on the roach that was dying as it waited for him to finish it off. The swirls of color in his mosaic of curved glass below mirrored itself in the sky that echoed above him. He was tripping with no need of LSD all over again, snatches of color billowing out along the side of his eyes like wings.

"Like Icarus, minus the wax that melted and messed his flight up." he muttered to himself proudly. He tilted in wind only he could feel as he sat up. His legs hung lazily over the terra cotta edge of the roof as he nursed a Heineken with a discarded cigarette floating in it, taking in his handiwork right- side up.

He hadn't discarded a bottle that he'd poured into his seemingly indestructible system since she'd gone, just added it to his masterpiece that bloomed in their old backyard.

The Angels posted around the edge of the roof implored the spirit in him to lay back down as he lumbered towards them to try and jump, the way he did every time the sun burnt a bit of the alcohol out of his blood. "No-I'm fine- I'm-" he slurred as they glared at him, jaws set to fight through yet another round.

He started to laugh harshly, "Angels- these Angels in

particular," he snorted as he referred to himself in third person, "trying to stop him from killing himself. When they sat there and did nothing when she-" His eyes cleared momentarily as he was smacked into sobriety by the vision of her sitting a few yards from him on the concrete in the center of the roof, cradling the baby that she took with her. Sobs overtook him.

"What do you care?" his vision of a heroin-bruised Mary holding their baby Jesus seethed. "You didn't love either of us! I killed us because you wouldn't leave!" she hissed. "Here! Have another drink on us so you won't forget why we're dead-" cackled the mother of the child she died with inside of her as she bowed her head. He blinked and nothing else was on the roof with him except the Angels assigned to stop him from killing himself and a pristine crate of Bombay Sapphire.

He laughed out loud again, shaking his head like it was just another joke pulled by his sentinels, his tears slicing through the air like daggers that the spiritual beings closest to him actually flinched from, reminding him of what he'd forgotten. "This IS a joke- you're taunting me! You're-" he sneered at the ring of Angels that began moving towards him. "It's not- I'm not the- her death was not my fault-" he laughed. "Their- their deaths-" he corrected himself as the clarity that tackled him in spurts rose up to its fullest glory.

In an instant he was charging through the Angels, his spiritual body near enough to the surface of his flesh to actually be able to make contact with them and physically fight through in a way he hadn't been able to before. In one swift duck, weave and dodge, he was more airborne than they'd ever allowed him to get, soaring up and through them, feeling the freedom of the pressure on his face as his body began to finally careen down through the five stories towards the meadow of glass.

"Anadyr! No-!!" boomed in the air around him, causing him to look up in shock right before his body made impact with the sea of glass and was slashed to ribbons, all save his impossibly perfect face, eyes glazed over with the impact of seeing his closest dream of what Heaven would be like open in the clouds right before him.

An angularly beautiful, incandescent woman surrounded in glinting spears, in a dress made of platinum d-rings holding out both arms to receive him was the last thing his 24 year old earthly eyes saw.

That's strange- this last frame tells us exactly who he is assigned to here," the ANCs said to one another telepathically as they peered into the perfectly preserved orbs of the slashed cadaver that was about to be recalibrated for entry into the Empyrean.

"Are you sure we shouldn't spool through his orbitals just to make sure he-" asked an ANC.

"We ALL know the mark of Third Council on sight. Why bother when it's been made that bluntly? No refractory reformation."

Another pair of Nephilim countered. They all agreed and began purifying what was left of him, reweaving all they could before grafts from Third Councilor's store of ethereal data were utilized.

chapter nineteen

Comptroller Yris slid into her viewing pod within the D/o theatre without speaking to the beings around her who also could not make it through a stretch of eternity without patching into the lives of those below and behind that kept them somehow spiritually sane. Her Holo-viewer rose up next to her left cheek as the wires of her heightened audio-assistance system snaked across her shoulders and slid into place against her eardrums.

"The Seer," she whispered internally, directing the holoviewer to the life that demanded her attention so violently. The worn face of the old lady she had run from the reflection of bloomed in front of the Comptroller's eyes. She peered at a storefront window at the base of a skyscraper where she had been left, on the edge of Hell's Kitchen a lifetime ago, through the reflection for something she would have never be able to explain if anyone had bothered to ask.

"Seer-" Comptroller Yris uttered, respectfully addressing the crone . The old lady latched onto the sound like a signal she'd been in search of. A soft smile spread across the woman's face.

"Be ready." The Seer that called herself Iris in hell on earth whispered to her reflection in the mirrored glass. "This is your only chance to free him. Do it."

Yris nodded as heat that was no longer supposed to be able to exist in her cheeks flooded up in the dark of the Demiourgos theatre complex.

chapter twenty

lalaaaala~Laalalaaaaa...

The little boy awoke to the sound of singing. He cautiously looked around. In one swift move he folded himself over the edge of the bed and peered under. Nothing.

lalaaaala~Laalalaaaaa... lalaaaala~Laalalaaaaa...

He tip-toed over and looked out on the fire escape through the bars. Sirens and street traffic blared outside, but no happily off-key singing. He knew he wasn't imagining it because if he was going to imagine singing, it wouldn't be all wobbly and girly.

He instantly made a game of it and stalked around the room like a tiger, wherever tigers went to hunt for other tigers. He was no longer in his mother's old room. Jungle sprung up all around him, territory he knew well. Trees he had scratched, rocks he had peed on in the past to mark his terrain .

He growled under his breath perfectly and sniffed the air as he heard it again.

lalaaaala~Laalalaaaaa...hahaha~ no he's not~ a little girl giggled to herself. The sound of it carried over the tops of the trees, slapped him on the forehead and right back into the room. He galloped around it in circles then stopped to catch his breath in front of the closet door mirror.

if you only knew/I can smell you~ she sang softly off-key and laughed to herself from somewhere inside of it. He tilted his head as he watched his reflection fade into a clump of reeds and cat-of-nine-tails that cloaked him from sight. He slowly reached up his hands to part them so he could see better.

About 20 feet on the other side of the mirror sprawled a little girl that he remembered but didn't know why. She was on a beige blanket spread atop a carpet that was a mottled mixture of blues and greens, drawing on big white paper with crayons that were spilled in every direction, crayons that suddenly started to float as the blanket turned to sand and the carpet to the blue- green water of a jungle stream.

if you only knew/I can smell you~laaaaaalaaaa- she stopped abruptly and looked in the direction of the reeds along the shore. A soft shy smile played across her lips before she cleared her throat and started to sing off-key again as if she'd sensed nothing.

The stream seemed to turn on itself in order to point out where he was hidden on her "island onto herself" she looked over the drawings she'd made that day pensively. Once the selection was made, she slid it into the water and watched it float in his direction out of the corner of her eye.

The little boy gently pulled his hands back towards himself. He shook his head in front of the mirror until his reflection came back and turned away. The jungle around him started to wilt.

The little girl giggled again and the foliage seemed to revive itself. He whipped around in time to see his reflection fade into reeds again and his feet get covered in water that lapped up onto the bank around him.

Right against his soaked sneakers floated a piece of paper with a drawing of a little boy with headphones and a superman cape on, standing on top of a pile of dead boys. Bewildered, he picked up the wet paper, folded it up and shoved it in his pocket before looking through the tall grass at her again. Suddenly there was a knock at the door. Both of them jumped.

"Gabryl, you alright in there? You been pretty quiet…"

The little boy darted to the door, opened it and whispered "I'm Okay, Gramma…"

"You sure honey?" his grandmother whispered.
"I'm Okay-"He grumbled, embarrassed. "I'm just playing jungle-"he whispered hoarsely. The little girl stood up on her tip-toes in the center of her island, trying to see through the mirror from her side.

"Okay," She sighed, taking her grandchild in her arms and hugging him. "I know you had a hard day, so I'm a leave you alone. I'll call you for dinner okay?" He nodded. "Now don't get lost out there in the Jungle," his grandmother whispered. "Cause me and your Gran-pere need you here with us for dinner tonight- He's coming home from work early just to have dinner with your dignified self,ok?"

"I'll be available" he blushed into the flesh of his Gramma's arm, suddenly excited about getting to see his Gran-pere before going to bed.

"Go head now, you probably got jungle folk waiting-" his grandmother whispered, swatting at his backside before she shut the door. She leaned her forehead against it momentarily and then walked to the kitchen. Her husband would be home shortly, and she hoped he knew how to get the boy to talk the way men can sometimes do.

Gabryl plowed back over to the mirror and saw nothing but himself. He tried to will the reeds to return, but it wouldn't. His face twisted up in silent rage as he plunked down on the floor in front of it.

The paper in his back pocket crumpled against him. His eyes got as big as saucers as he nervously pulled out the still damp picture that had been floated across the river to him by the little girl. He unfolded it again. It was only at the second glance that he noticed one more person drawn into the picture. A little girl off in the corner of the page with a red cape on too, and a thought bubble over her head that said "Yay!!"

He smiled for the first time all day then sat and stared at the pretty picture for hours. When he heard his Gran-pere come across the threshold, he folded it up, stuck the picture up under his tee shirt for safekeeping then tucked his shirt back into his pants.

chapter twenty one

Little Anukai kept drawing. Scattered everywhere were plans held down against the wind by carefully placed handfuls of sand. The island seemed to grow smaller the longer she stayed there, the older she somehow got that didn't show in this place. But she didn't care. This was the closest to home she had.

She felt like she'd been at it forever, sitting in the center of maps, drafts, blueprints. Crows cawed overhead and butterflies danced in the torrent of energy that drifted up through the messy curls at the crown of her head with each smile that they all were closer to it finally being done. Nothing in her world was different after the little boy showed up on the shore. The reeds waved in cool breezes on the hot ever-after day and salamanders sunned on rocks she'd strung around the edge of her island. The waterfall behind her fell cheerfully over the carp that played tag under the surface of the water. To little Anukai his presence was proof that she was almost done.

At last, she pulled herself up and began to put the drawings into order, absently tossing the handfuls of sand that had been securing them against the wind over her shoulder. She sat down crosslegged as she flipped through them pensively. Butterflies nibbled on the nettles she'd tucked behind her ear in order to train them to remain encamped around her. Anukai scratched at her chin, contemplating how these plans would fit with the things already hidden in the woods, grown from a piece of red clay found in her pocket after a nap. She stretched the muscles in her neck that had tightened due to being hunched for so long, stood up and noticed the spread of water between her and the shore as if for the first time.

She always forgot she couldn't swim until it was time to cross back. She threw her head back and began to bawl at the prospect of being trapped on her island unto herself forever.

chapter twenty two

"Dinner~" His Gramma sung out.

Gabryl snapped out of the silent revelry he'd been lost in. The notes of sound he had been seeing from the inside hovered above him in a tangled cloud of symbols he didn't get that he understood.

He waited and listened to his Gran-pere across the hall as the stoic gentleman washed his hands and face after work. Gabryl knew that he'd worked doubles for days as a foreman at a nearby sugar factory, but no matter how tired he had to have been, he would not disrespect his wife's table by not changing clothes for dinner. He even shaved.

Gabryl used to think it was crazy until he'd seen his Gramma flinch at the kiss on the cheek he customarily gave her one night he didn't. Gabryl had sat as this Titan in his mind's eye lumbered through dinner and no amount of praise from his lips over the food or her beauty made a dent in her melancholy demeanor. Gabryl played with his peas without reprimand in the first uncomfortable silence he'd ever experienced in the presence of the two. On that night, when Gramma stood up to clear dishes and retrieve dessert, Gran-pere had politely excused himself to the bathroom, motioning to Gabryl to get up and help her clear the table. Gabryl remembered that night in detail because it had been the last time she'd made peanut butter layer pie- his favorite- as a surprise, and he'd spent an extra five minutes squealing and screaming.

"You made my pie?! Why didn't you tell me we were going to have *my* pie?" He had wrapped around his grandmother's legs.

"-Stop it boy, or it's going to end up on the floor-"

"I'd eat it anyway- it's still my pie! And your floors are clean-"

By the time she had wiggled him off her, a good ten minutes had passed. As his Grandmother had tried to arrange the dessert in the center of the table, slapping at his hands as they playfully grabbed for it, his Gran-pere had quietly walked back into the dining room.

"She made my *pie~ my*" Gabryl had sung up to his grandfather, then noticed the two little red and white shreds of paper stuck to his cheek. "What happened to your face?"

The stern smile of his grandmother had softened as she looked over at her husband. Gabryl stepped back a little in surprise as her eyes had caught fire and, for the first time ever, Gabryl saw what had to have been his grandfather's version of a blush as he leaned gently in and kissed his wife again, the smoothness of his cheek completely chasing away what had been there during dinner.

"What are y'all doing-" he had asked, almost alarmed.
"I'm being kind to my wife-" His grandfather had murmured as he nuzzled her ear in front of the little boy.

"Well, can I have pie while you being all 'kind'?" He'd fussed, then slammed his hand over his mouth.

"Pie never trumps wife-" his grandfather had playfully growled and popped the little boy in the head as fast as quicksilver.

Gabryl laughed to himself as he realized he still didn't know how the old man had been able to even get over there that fast. He had remembered the swat, but he remembered every bite of pie even more.

The sound of the water in the sink tonight made Gabryl's head a little less foggy as he stood up and shook off the notes that still tried to stick to his crown. He opened the bedroom door a crack to see the yellow light of the bathroom across the way, the hands of his Gran-pere covered in soap bubbles. His grandfather leaned forward as he felt the piercing eyes of his grandson imploring him to play peek-a-boo. They caught each other's eyes and grinned.

"Are you rushing me, son?" His grandfather asked with a larger version of the gravelly voice the boy heard when he opened his own mouth.

"I gotta wash my hands too-" the little boy giggled.

His grandfather nodded, said " *oh- I see~* " and dried his hands before holding the door open for the boy to venture across the hall and dive into the sunny bathroom. At the last minute Gabryl entangled himself in his grandfather's legs as if trying to knock him down and was swung up towards the large man's shoulders.

He wrapped his arms around his Gran-pere's neck and planted a big wet kiss on his cheek before he ordered the old man to put him down as if he couldn't bear the intimacy and scampered in to wash his hands. His grandfather made his way to the kitchen to find out what had happened that day at school in detail.

As Gabryl lathered his hands with rose-scented soap crying started to echo around him. He whirled around, confused, before coming back to the mirror again. Inside the little girl stood on the edge of her island wailing at the top of her lungs.

He looked around at the bathroom on his side of the mirror and then whispered "-why are you crying?" His voice echoed over her head loud enough to make her cries dry up to a sniffle.

"I'm stuck!" she cried out softly.

"But-How did you get there?"

"I can't remember-" she sniffed.
"Why not just swim?" he asked simply.
"I don't remember how- and bad stuff happens in water-"

Gabryl looked at the world surrounding her and saw the little land-bridge of sand strung up between the island and the shore to the far left of her. He blinked because he hadn't seen it there the last time. "That over there looks like it leads to the shore-" he whispered, motioning to it.

She looked over her shoulder and saw the land-bridge of sand she hadn't realized she'd tossed behind her. She looked back at the sky and blushed as she gingerly stepped out on it.

"I didn't see that-" she whispered sheepishly, an edge of confidence on her voice now that the problem was solved. "Will you come play with me?" she whispered as she sat on the shore, flustered at the request having fell so easily from her bee-stung lips.

Now it was his turn to blush. Before he could answer, his grandmother called out for dinner again.

chapter twenty three

Little Anukai kneeled by the bank of the river to wait.

Butterflies swarmed above her, creating a lattice of brightly colored wings as her salamanders swam up onto the shore and marched around her, sentinels on land watch. A melange of brightly-hued birds sung out a lullaby in unison from nearby bushes and trees.

As her eyelids got heavier, she sleepily noticed the little air bubbles of the army of goldfish just under the surface in case an attack was attempted by sea.

A gaunt old, translucent man hobbled out of the nearby forest and sat down next to the domed amphitheater of butterflies that enclosed the little girl.

"Show me where I come from again, Diaz" the little girl sleepily mumbled to the Guardian who had been away for so Long. The butterflies and salamanders parted so he could see into the hive if he so pleased.

"I will-" an emaciated Vayo Kahn Diaz whispered. "I will-"

chapter twenty four

"...show me where I come from again, Diaz-" Her voice echoed around his head.

Vayo Kahn Diaz sat on a stone bench and stared off into the waterfall beyond the arrival pools at the center of the Empyrean imperial gardens. His eyes were rimmed with quicksilver tears he wasn't supposed to be able to produce as he fought to stay zoned out enough to hear her. He couldn't think about what she had to have gone through down there. How much damage had been done to her since he'd disappeared. But most of all, he couldn't think about what it took for her not to feel as abandoned by him as she was by every one else. The word to describe what shook his chest was Guilt.

"Stop worrying, I'm fine." She mumbled groggily. "I'm strong, remember? Strong enough to see you-" She yawned, "Even sleep. Even now... SO~ bring me home...Come on! Come on-come-on-" She kept needling him in his own mind.

"Enough-" Diaz growled, sounding like his old self for the first time in eons.

Diaz got up off the bench and looked around as he walked across the stone terrace, feet not touching the ground until he was well past the hushed arrivals zone area. His toes glided above the lotus culverts that curved away from the present pools like forgotten fault-lines, into the well-tended trees and burning bushes that were the closest to the Leuce the citizens and denizens of the Empyrean were unofficially allowed to get.

Eventually Vayo Kahn Diaz pulled his legs up into himself while still standing tall and sunk into himself until he was levitating about ten inches up off the ground.

The foliage shifted to reveal the worn remnants of an old wall with a doorway cut into it. Each of the huge stones in it fit together without mortar. Through the doorframe was an ancient infinity pool, visible through the shoved aside slabs over it. He floated across the threshold and sat down in front of the pool. The surrounding chunks of marble and stone seemed to press away from his presence, as if the place made room for his breath.

The view of the overgrown abyss was breath-taking. Vivid greens scratched against each other under the heavy red sky. It saturated to a deeper green the farther you looked down if you could fight past the vertigo. The ravine tumbled down until it simply bled to the black of all other abysses. Stretches of silver smudges were simply the reflection of low-flying clouds his eyes were no longer wired to see.

"Come-" Diaz whispered across water that seemed to froth up then spill down into the landscape. A swarm of butterflies shot up from deep within the abyss and hovered over the Bethesda pool in the shape of a figure eight.

chapter twenty five

Little Anukai woke with a start at the whoosh of her butterflies moving away from her.

"Hey-!" she tried to cry out as she shuffled the crayons in her pocket so they'd stop pressing into her hip. Only one tiny monarch butterfly seemed to notice in the midst of its ascent, turned on its wings and coasted back down through the thick air, landing gently against her throat.

"Oh~" she whispered as the cries caught inside of her evaporated with the beating of each fragile wing.

A slow smile spread across her face as she exploded into shimmering dust that was caught up in the wake of the butterflies towards the red sky.

chapter twenty six

"Show me your hands-" His grandmother directed when little Gabryl sat down at the table. He looked sheepishly at his grandfather as she inspected them.

"I washed them-" he said, incredulous at what was being insinuated.
"Ot!" she snapped severely, stopping him mid-sentence."Just making sure."

General Gramma consulted with Corporal Gran- pere, who gave a small nod.

She lifted up the polished silver dome that hid Dinner, with a capital D. Chicken and rice, gandules, collard greens and kale. He ate like he'd not eaten in days, which was almost the truth. About two mornings ago, His mom had left him with a box of Captain Crunch cereal and the Television as she'd headed out to drop his little brother off at the special-care facility she often stuck the boy into when he was too much for her to handle.

He hadn't seen her when he'd come home or gotten up the following day, and had moved through his days on quiet auto-pilot until the fight at school today. He knew they were plying him with food to prime him to talk, but he didn't care, because he knew how his Gramma loved him by how she stood up to his mother. He knew he could talk and they'd understand.

Besides, with all his favorite foods glistening back at him from the center or the table, everything set up like it was Christmas, a tiny voice in the back of his mind wondered if there might be peanut butter pie coming his way too.

By the time he finished his second plate, his grandfather had cleared his throat in a way that let Gabryl know it was time to say something.

"I hate that school." Was the only thing that his brain could think to say, followed by "My momma hates me...but you love me. I know you love me. Can I live with you?"

"Why do you hate school, Son?" his grandfather asked him Plainly.

"I don't hate School-" he sighed," I hate that one...cause," Gabryl started softly, "They all hate me!"

He pushed his plate away from him a bit and put hit elbows up on the table. They knew a torrent was only going to fly out of the quiet little boy if they let it come out of him the way it wanted to. He sighed angrily.

"First they hated me because I was small, and used to pick on me!" he started. "Then they hated me more when they found out I was smart, because of those dumb tests the teacher made us took!"

"Take-" His Gramma corrected out of habit.
"-Take. And then..." his voice trailed off and he seemed to get lost inside of himself right in front of them. His head drooped and he appeared to be trying to stare through the wounds still healing on his chest that occasionally itched. Tears slid down his cheeks. His grandmother looked as if she were going to leap across the table and pull him into her arms, but he looked up at her like a wounded bird and then over at his grandfather.

"Come here, son," His Gran-pere whispered and held his hand out to him. The little boy crawled up into his grandfather's lap and cried into the starchy fabric of his Guyanabana shirt as the old man rocked him back and forth in his arms. He wouldn't wipe at the tears because he didn't want the boy to grown up like he did, thinking there was something wrong with having to cry from time to time.

Gran-pere's first tears had fallen exactly sixteen days after the sudden death of his own overworked father about thirty years ago. When Gabryl started to speak again, he was woozy from the sheer exhaustion of having had a good cry.

"Then," he started again, "the teachers told everybody I was.. .was bad because--- -said that what happened to me happened to boys who talk to strangers- and everybody hated me more. I didn't mean to be - I-and- But mama says it too." He hiccuped. "When she- she's the real her- she says the same-when she's- you know-" he looked down and hiccuped again.

Shaking, his grandfather took his chin in his hand and tilted the boy's face up towards him so he could look him in the eyes. "You are **not** a bad boy. In fact, you're the best man I've met in a long time-" the old man chuckled sincerely, his eyes welled up with tears.

"It's not your fault-" the old man's voice shook with fervor. "What that evil, sick man did to you...was- Is not and will never be your fault-Your mother knows it, but she's hiding from what her mess led to-"

Gabryl whimpered in pain as if the truth of it hurt him even more than the lies adults had spoken into him.

"Your mother is Wrong, Baby!" His Grandmother echoed

hoarsely a beat behind her husband as tears streamed down her face, thanking God that Danise wasn't there to tempt the Baptist out of her due to the damage her addiction continued to do.

"I'm not bad?" he whispered.

His Gran-pere whispered "Nope," with authority, repeatedly, until he saw in the little boy's eyes that he was starting to believe it. His Gramma started saying it in unison with her husband as she came over and wrapped her arms around the both of them.

"If he stays here, he's in another school district, honey- and Danise is... just a-" Her husband looked up at her and nodded.

"We'll start taking care of everything in the morning, I'll even call off work-" he whispered as he kissed his grandson on the forehead in affirmation. "Okay- so it's settled. You alright now, son?" Gabryl smiled shyly and nodded, elated that he was already home. "Then go eat like a man! I only saw you handle two plates over there! You a growing boy! You can do better than that! This is your Gramma's cooking, son!"

Gabryl scampered back over to his own seat and held out his plate towards the center of the table, a self-confident grin plastered across his salt-streaked cheeks. Gramma put smaller servings of each portion on his plate.

"Hey-!" he called out as she raised her hand to silence him. "But I want- I'm growing!"

"Gabryl..." she murmured flirtatiously."there's pie-"

He fell back in his seat still holding the plate, swooning from the mere mention of the word. His eyes dramatically rolled about in his head, blessed. Then his bottomless pit of a stomach growled and he jumped back to the business of clearing the plate at hand. By the time pie hit and he hit back, he was in a daze. He wandered back to his mother's old room, crawled into bed and fell out.

chapter twenty seven

Butterfly wings deposited the dust of her on the craggy slope just over the ledge of the veranda Diaz waited on. The wind blew her back together as she climbed over rocks and clefts as if she had hind's feet.

When he saw her little head peek over the horizon line of the pool, he didn't know if the ground shook from the force of silent joy that exploded out of her or him.

She leapt up and immediately turned to dust again, particles of joy that the wind blew into him, coating him with her spirit before she re-materialized in his arms, hugging him for real for the first time ever. Quicksilver trickled down his eyes as she looked up at him happily, knowing she was somehow seeing with her eyes who she had always only heard with them before.

"Hey, I thought you said you were a Black Mexican-" she meowed accusatorily as her irises dissolved into the whites of her eyes due to the atmospheric pressure. The little girl and her Guardian Angel hugged for an eternity.

"I was once-but that was before it was called Mexico-" he growled huskily into her wild little head of hair.

"You didn't answer when I sung to you-for like Forever!" Anukai whispered into the cool flesh of her Guardian's neck.

"I couldn't-" Diaz croaked as a silvery tear slid slowly down his cheek. As it splattered against her forehead she morphed back into a cloud of gold and copper dust that collapsed into nothingness within his arms.

He dared not blink against the sudden coat of grit on his eyes nor inhale the zephyrs that gently rose up to play with a new friend, scattering microscopic portions of her spirit over the slabs of stone that surrounded them. The subatomic systems at the core of her spun around him in pockets like draydels of dust. His face began to itch as it dawned on him that she was what he was trying not to look through. She giggled, caught up in play with the wind.

When he could no longer resist, his lids slowly closed. His heart throbbed in his ears as the red of the sky was replaced by the even more intense red inside his eyes, watering against who was trapped in them. An explosion of white went off inside of his head, he howled and everything spun out of control into more and more white-hot light.

Little Anukai started to crack up and gently tugged on his ear.

Diaz warily raised his left brow and felt a breeze against his face again. The itch and burn of his eyes was replaced with the sensation of splashed water. His eyes snapped open and his body jumped, stunned by the intensity of the surroundings, hands out in front of him as if to brace himself against impact, totally bewildered. Diaz grunted in shock as it registered that his hands were the color of cinnamon again. Anukai was wrapped around his head, legs dangling over his shoulders, giggling like a little monkey in his ear.

"How-where the-what did you do?!-" He stammered, trying to reach around to grab at her. She giggled more, but said nothing. Each time he missed her, his hands flew back in front of his face as if his arms were on a tight spring and he marveled at the returned ferocity of his coloring. "Anukai- What- what did you do, child? Answer me-" he whispered.

She hiccupped as her laughter softened and her voice hitched in her throat. "We flew...you jumped - why did you close your eyes?" she whispered shyly.

Hit by vertigo, Diaz spun around 360 degrees, as a mountain of yellow and light green seemed to rise up behind him as far up as he could see. His eyes grappled against the hills of wheat in search of more red sky until he found a snatch of it. A silvery lowflying cloud condensed up directly over them and floated off in the direction he'd initially faced when they'd first landed. They were in the Leuce. The Badlands. Off in the distance, a grove of obscenely tall Aspens reached up towards the green that faded back up to red, calling the newly created quicksilver cloud to the tops of leaves that shimmered gold and white in the glare of the sky.

Residuals from the leap they'd taken together cut into his mind's eye, viewed from the shadow of himself as it advanced forward with the jumps and starts of a hand-held flipbook. There were no foot-prints in the shimmering dust that coated the terrace between the shadow and them, only tiny splashes of water from the tips of Diaz's toes as they skimmed across the surface of the infinity pool with the happy child tucked behind his head like she was diving into the deep end of the pool, not bothering to think whether she was safe or not because of who she was with. Laughter exploded out of her as they sailed into the golden green abyss below, his shadow taking them in as they spiraled down in the heavy atmosphere. As Diaz's body shifted to instinctively slow the force, Anukai, still screaming like she was in the front car of a roller-coaster intuitively tucked her head into the crook of his shoulder. Jumping felt like flying, flying felt like falling through clouds that went from icy to hot as they passed through them. Diaz landed like a pro, as if he'd been free-falling in every life he'd ever lived.

Anukai was still screaming from joy that Diaz couldn't hear until his shadow had caught up with them on the ground and tickled the soles of her feet with its presence. He shook the recall off in amazement."How did you know we'd-" Diaz started softly.

"I didn't jump, you did, silly-didn't he?" Anukai laughed, looking over at his shadow as if she expected his shadow to somehow nod in agreement. She crawled around to the front of him, tucked into the sling of his arms, then became restless after hearing the triplicate beating of his heart. "Put me down." As she hit the ground, she instantly looped her fingers around his and pulled him forward.

"...Where are we going, Anukai?" Diaz whispered.

"I have to show you something. In there-" she said as she pointed toward the woods.

chapter twenty eight

Gabryl woke from his sugar-shock induced sleep with a start. He peered through the darkness at the clock on the windowsill next to the bed. It was eleven thirty. He slammed his hand over his mouth as a gasp rose up, aware that his grandparents were knocked out by nine-thirty or ten.

His lust for pie had totally wiped the rendezvous with the little girl in the mirror from his mind. Distraught, he climbed out of bed and tip-toed across the hall to the bathroom and shut the door in the dark, shoving a towel against the bottom of the door before he flipped on the light. The sunny yellow paint, towels and curtains of the little room made it seem like it was still midday. Gabryl climbed up on the toilet, then the sink and silently stared into the mirror, waiting without a word. He saw nothing but his own reflection.

"She probably thinks I stood her up, but I didn't mean to- I just fell asleep and-" chased its tail around the center of his forehead, imploring him to open his mouth to make it stop.

He reached over, latched the door , turned back off the light and waited in the dark, using all that he had in him not to think he was crazy. Even when pitch-black, the bathroom smelled sunny like a rose garden. He began fiddling with the hem of his pants when the tiny folded sheet of paper that had sweated to his stomach as he slept crinkled. He pulled it out and unfolded it gingerly in the dark, squinting his eyes to follow the wobbly lines of it as he traced the wax with his fingers.

Absently, he put the drawing up on the mirror and pressed it out of boredom, then went back to fiddling with it instead in his lap, unaware of the momentary shift in the dark shadows reflected in the mirror.

He startled a bit when he realized a lot more wax than he recalled seemed to be on the paper, and reached over to turn back on the light to inspect it again.

"What the-" Gabryl's eyes bugged out of his head as the picture had become one of trees and giants and a woman who looked like a spider in a tree with a man whose head stuck out of what looked like a cocoon. Bewildered, he slammed off the light, hopped down off the sink and put the bath towel back where it belonged. When he gently opened the bathroom door again and headed back to bed, his head was flooded with the memory of the little girls voice.

"I'll come get you-got any sweets? I never get to eat sweets-and I don't know how to make them-here-" Something in him believed her even more when he heard her inside his own head. He pivoted on the cream carpet in the hallway and tip- toed to the kitchen.

As he folded the picture back up and shoved it back under his tee shirt, he had the sneaking suspicion that he should bring more than peanut butter pie, in case he didn't want to share "or maybe she doesn't like peanut butter, everybody doesn't like peanut butter-" he reasoned to himself. In addition to the last slice of pie Gabryl grabbed four big oatmeal raisin cookies "...just in case she always had to eat two-" like he did.

He tip-toed back to his room and looked around wondering what he should do while he waited. The bright-coloured quilt his grandmother had crocheted for his mom a long time ago was shoved into the wall. Even though he mostly hated her, keeping the quilt on the bed was the only show of love and forgiveness he had in him to give. Most days he woke to find it balled up and thrown across the room in his sleep. Methodically, he placed the plate with the pie and cookies on the floor in front of the mirror, then turned and pulled all the bedding onto the floor to make a nest there too, so she wouldn't miss him if she ever came back. He laid down and placed a pillow on his head and squeezed, hoping that the pressure would make him not think. Restless on the floor, he pulled the drawing out again to look at it in the dark. It was still trees and two little kids with giants and a spider-woman.

Gabryl sighed and inattentively crawled out of his nest to place the drawing up against this mirror too, but this time he left it there and crawled back into his knot of blankets on the floor. He put the pillow over his head again and grumbled "-I know she didn't leave me," as he fell back asleep not really against his will, oblivious to the vista of trees on the shore as it came into view in the mirror. As his mouth slackened against the pillow, the little girl in the forest on the other side of the mirror started to sing.

chapter twenty nine

Diaz and Anukai walked deeper into a forest that seemed to have sprung up out of nowhere. Invigorated, he took in huge draughts of air with his mouth, letting the blackened dust embedded in his lungs to exist above trickle out of his nose.

The little girl danced around her Guardian amongst trees whose leaves glistened with the colors of a perpetual Indian summer farther above their heads. She sang in syllables that made no sense to any tongue but hers as her heart bounded with joy at being reunited with her long lost friend. The only one she'd ever felt she'd had. He hummed alongside her, songs she didn't realize he'd taught her on her darkest days below.

"We're here-" She sang.
"Where?" Diaz whispered, mystified.
"My *Sanctuary*!" she sang out, giddy from finally showing it to someone. "Look what *I* did-" she trilled as she gave him the tour.

The copse of trees opened to an area of new growth. Trees that ranged from barely four feet to eight feet high had been meticulously planted in a rectangle beneath the boughs of much older aspens that had been planted in a circle. A path led around the new growth and back out into the woods to a smaller circle of wizened silver and black trunks.

To each trunk was nailed a piece of beat-up cardboard on which Anukai had drawn an image of a happy little girl in a different state of play, with herself, or with friends she imagined she'd have, even kids of her own.

 She walked him to each one, going on and on in detail about the life she was going to lead, the dreams she was going to have anyway. In spite of. He listened to her intently.

"You're in the one over there, with the long-haired lady who watches my sanctuary for me when I'm away," she said as she pointed over her shoulder to the tree that they'd not yet gotten to. His brows went up at the sound of "long-haired Lady" but he just as quickly dismissed the strange comment. His eyes rested on the grass.

Nestled in it was a less confident drawing of her neck draped in all kinds of brightly coloured rings, with a crown nestled on her stick-figure head. It was the only one laying at the base of a tree. Diaz bent down in the grass and focused on the wobbly lines and the wobbly smile on the girl, and space saved to the left in the unfinished picture. He looked at Anukai and peered into her eyes, questioning her about who she was saving space for without saying a word. Anukai blushed and looked away.

"He's not here yet, but he's coming to play with me today, and I wanna draw him right," she whispered.

"He?" Diaz asked, curious." Who is *HE*?"

"He's my other – other iono what he is- but he plays with me sometimes- when you left-and- Well not yet, iono. But I know I want to draw it right, because-"

Diaz had never seen the little girl flustered before. A huge smile spread across his face as he tried to put two and two together. *Anukai has a boyfriend?* He sang out softly inside of himself.

He caught himself before any teasing rose up and shut down what was trying to spill from her mouth and put a serious look on his face. "Because?" He encouraged her to continue.

"Because we win. We both do. Stop looking at me like that!" She said simply.

"Like what?!" he bellowed heartily, a look of mock confusion replacing the overtly serious one.

"Just because you didn't tease me with your mouth doesn't mean it's not spilling out of your eyes," she said precociously. Diaz hugged her. "I told you I was okay-" she grumbled into his arm-pit. "I told you-"

"When do I get to see your whatever he is?" Diaz laughed softly.

She growled "And don't start crying either-" she muttered softly. " I have to go get him," she whispered, "...but- But I wanted you to see here first-"

Diaz hugged her even tighter. "Lemme go-" Diaz moaned as if tired of her. She swatted at him and hugged him even tighter, then pulled away and started singing again.

But this time, Diaz knew she wasn't singing any song he'd taught her. He swatted her on the bottom as she ran off into the woods towards the river.

"Don't leave," she ordered over her shoulder.
"Where would I go without you?" He called after her as he settled against the base of the tree nearest him. His eyes began to flicker as he took in every texture around him, lulled to a state of drowsiness for the first time in eons.

chapter thirty

Kahn was too over-stimulated to notice the sheer tendrils of long hair that slowly crawled down the trunk towards his face or the beautiful woman perched in the boughs overhead, just as translucent as the hair that danced towards him like the tentacles of a jellyfish. A strand played in the black smoke that dribbled out of his mouth as he slept for the first time in forever.

"She" peered intently into his face from above, tattooing every plane of it on the inside of her eyes over the one that had faded away in the midst of forever. Just as her ghostly hair was about to make contact with him, a spiritual dog-whistle of sorts erupted off in the distance, causing her to yank her head up out of adoration into fight mode, the antique copper monocle she kept nestled behind her ear flying from its roost into place in front of her eye.

"Punishers, yes?" she growled to herself. "Trolling for combat in the Leuce? Good, I was getting a bit hungry-" "She" threw her head back and laughed manically on mute as the monocle flew back behind her ear. A wicked smile spread across her translucent cheeks as the rest of her never-ending hair danced under tree-tops and down trunks, a force-field like veil of hair swathing the little girl's sanctuary in plain sight.

"She" looked back down at Diaz, her once-beloved, and somersaulted out of the uppermost branches of the tree in slow motion, gently coasting down to him on her own hair as the Punishers came closer to what would be his horizon line from the ground. Her hair pooled around him at the base of the tree.

Her left arm reached out lovingly towards his torso, Balinese metal fingernails extended in a mudra of love as she swiftly bent her elbow and nestled the love of many lifetimes into a sleeperhold, orgasmic over the sensation of touching him, even as almost nothing more than a spirit.

Oblivious, Diaz, shuffled in arms he didn't even sense as she nuzzled the side of his face gingerly, taking his color onto her with every inhalation next to his head. The Punishers shot off another whistle, this one on his frequency on the ground, and he awoke with a start, the weight of Her hair draped across his entire frame heavily, trapping him in case he'd even thought to move.

"sSssssHhhhhh~" she whispered erotically into his ear. His head swiveled as much as it could in the hold and he almost yelled out as he caught sight of the ghost of the love of his life, who promptly slammed her hand over his mouth and flicked her eyes over to his right as shush was communicated between the two of them.

"HiyaBayh~" she slurred into the softness of the only place she'd ever felt she'd belonged.

Before he could think to do otherwise, Diaz was overwhelmed by the smell of her he'd kept with him after all this time as she slid her tongue across his mouth between her sheer fingers.

The impact of the kiss knocked color back into her as her hair folded just below her shoulders before it angled back up into the trees.

"Kago-I" He stammered, the gray irises of his eyes rising up to the surface with the rest of every aspect of himself that had been canceled out as no longer necessary above.

"Not exactly Kago anymore, and I'm surprised you recall that name-but...I know," she whispered gently, amazed at the life-force returned to her with just one kiss from him. She cleared her throat.

"You seem to have some company on your ass." the ghost of his wife whispered to a bewildered Diaz.

"At least a retinue, looking for little old you-did you think they wouldn't notice when their master builder jumped ship again?"

Diaz looked over to his right and "Fuck" slipped out of his lips under the cup of her hand.

"Exactly." She purred as she lowered herself all the way down and straddled his lap. "But only If you insist~" she whispered. A fully saturated Kagome Arachne leaned in for another lick, her hair stealthily pulling two of them back up into the upper boughs of the trees.

The end.

ABOUT THE AUTHOR

Author and multimedia artist Angel Brynner has marched to the beat of her
own drum across the arts for over two decades. After formal training with
the vanguard of the menswear industry she helmed her own line of men's
clothing and produced events for the collection in the club scenes of
New York and Tokyo.

She became quietly known for the futuristic cautionary tales back-dropping
her collections, taking over clubs and the guerilla-marketing style she used
to slam her vision into the hearts of her fans. While being sponsored by
Multinational companies desiring audience with her underground tribe, she
returned from Japan to her hometown to press charges against a pedophile
before the statute of limitations ran out.

Cast as a vigilante by a corrupt sex crimes unit for trying to protect another
child from the same attacker, during the media onslaught against
the first brave adults to come forward and press charges against
the Catholic priests that had abused them as children she was hit with a
vision of all those already lost in a sick war on kids no one talked about.

She committed herself & her art to doing something about it.

The grievechronic universe was forged in the fires of imagining the
Armageddon that would erupt through a generation of kids who
had finally had enough abuse at the hands of adults and
banded together under their grievances.
The epic spiritual, metaphysical, and historical implications
of such an event played out on every level- from the hellish norms
that caused it to what would be called heaven by such a broken world-
made her head spin.

Published by Kokopellima Press, each free-standing installment of grievechronic
Is a take-no- prisoners tale.

Alongside AOLAB[the active-art series featuring the multimedia work
that fed Eutaxis, Ecclesia, Exodus, Erebus, Exist and the kinetic collection
of novels that follow them], Angel Brynner's books are the culmination of
an artistic journey many years in the making,
all leading to a mysterious future project entitled **Transcendence.**

Eutaxis. /Grievechronic\...
Angel Brynner
2h 44m

ECCLESIA. /grievechronic...
Angel BRYNNER
3h 3m

EXODUS. /grievechronic\...
Angel BRYNNER
2h 21m

EREBUS./grievechronic\...
Angel Brynner
2h 56m

EXIST. /grievechronic\ boo...
Angel Brynner
2h 36m

ESTHESIS. /grievechronic...
Angel Brynner
3h 47m

THE NINTH (& LATEST) ENTRY TO THE / GRIEVECHRONIC\ UNIVERSE

False utopias look like heaven when they exist inside of you, but the spell breaks when you fall. Halcyon days harbor great space for healing if they can stand being held up to the light. The memories we run and hide in may overlap or coincide, but underneath each pleasing space is all that we have yet to face. Hiding bodies to embrace the good is par for the course. But those bones must live again in order to truly break free. The good goes down in spite of what you have to ignore to be grateful for it, but ignoring shit doesn't make anything really go away.…and going away only goes so far.

"It looks like Heaven." That may be true. But don't forget what you've gone through

Elysum

before or after the fall may never have been Paradise at all.

ISBN 978-1-950077-83-0

52000

9 781950 077830

Angel Brynner
ELYSIUM
/grievechronic\
Now available in paperback
Everywhere.

www.ingramcontent.com/pod-product-compliance
Lightning Source LLC
Chambersburg PA
CBHW040533170726
48295CB00012B/450